FOOD

French Bread
PIZZA

VILLAINS

AVALANCHIA
Dr. Pangea

VILLAIN

NINJA-000

Street Angel

NAME: Jesse Sanchez (aka: Deadliest Girl Alive, Shiraz Thunderbird, Princess of Poverty, Trash Can)
FIRST APPEARANCE: Street Angel mini-comic

Jesse has the powers of the ultimate ninja but the intelligence, attitude, and will of a 13 y.o. girl. With h[er] trusty skateboard and ability to eat nearly anything, the streets of Wilksboro are more or less safe unless she has school or is distracted - then anything goes.

21 FUN FACT: Jesse does not like school.

SERPENTINA

VILLAIN

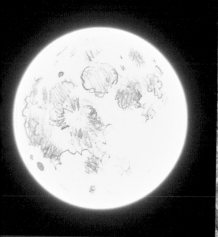

MOON!

VILLAIN

RODENTIA

VILLAIN

AN
$20.63

VAN MAN

WITCH

BLACK ALICE

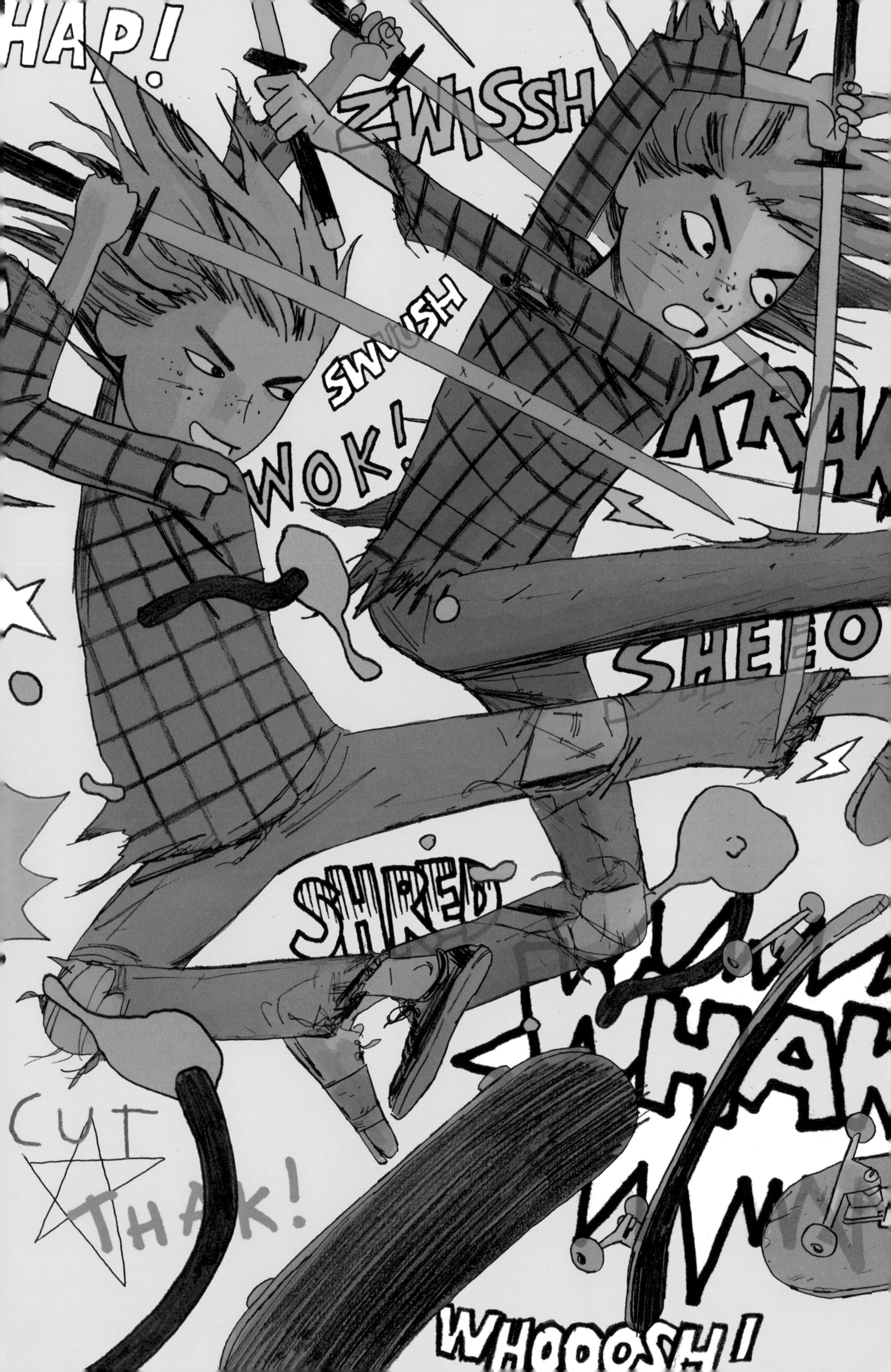
HAP!
ZWISSH
SWISH
WOK!
SHRED
CUT
THAK!
WHOOOSH!

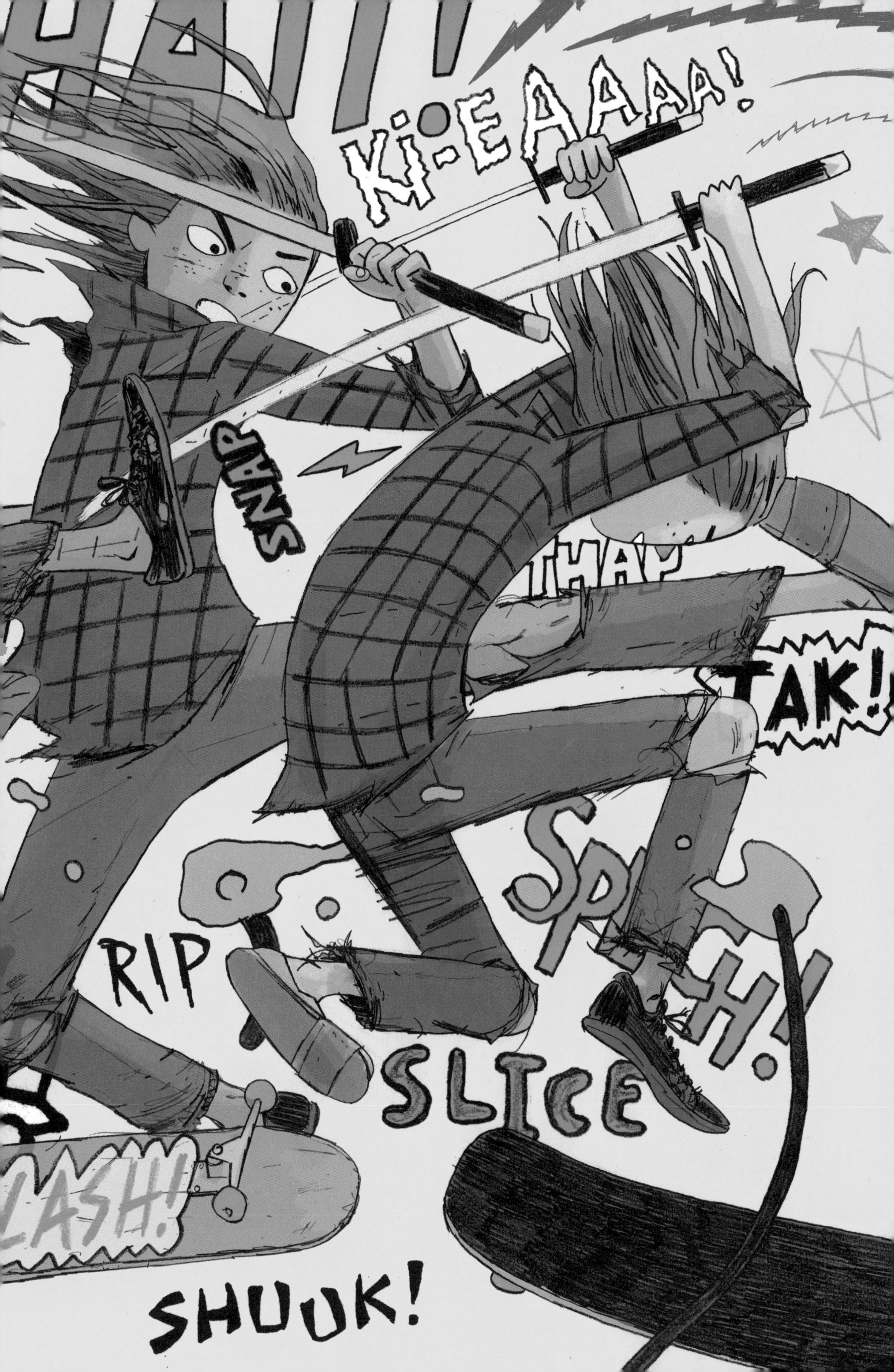
KI-EAAAA!
SNAP
THAP
TAK!
RIP
SLICE
SHUUK!

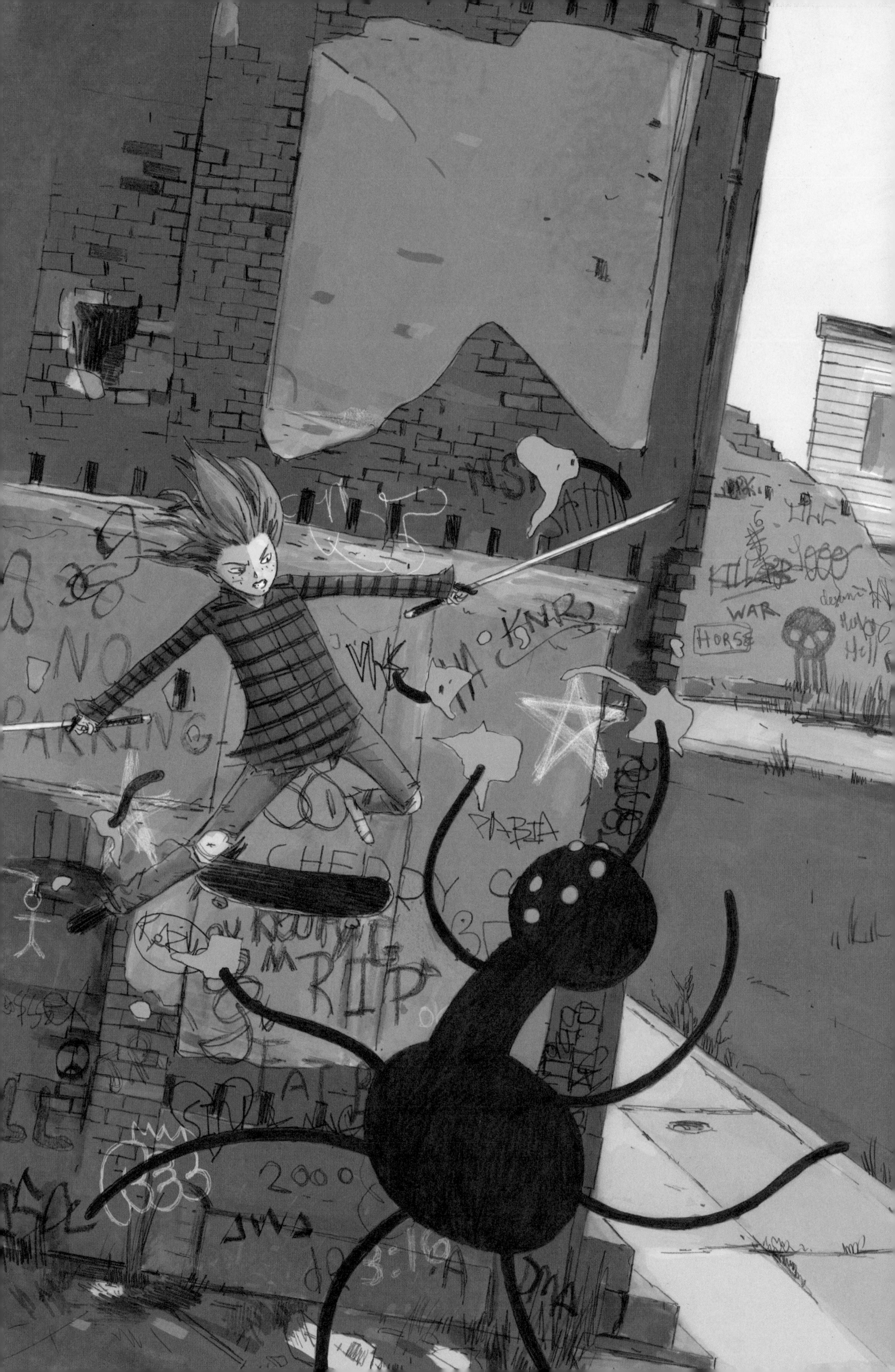
NO
PARKING
WAR
HORSE
RIP
2000

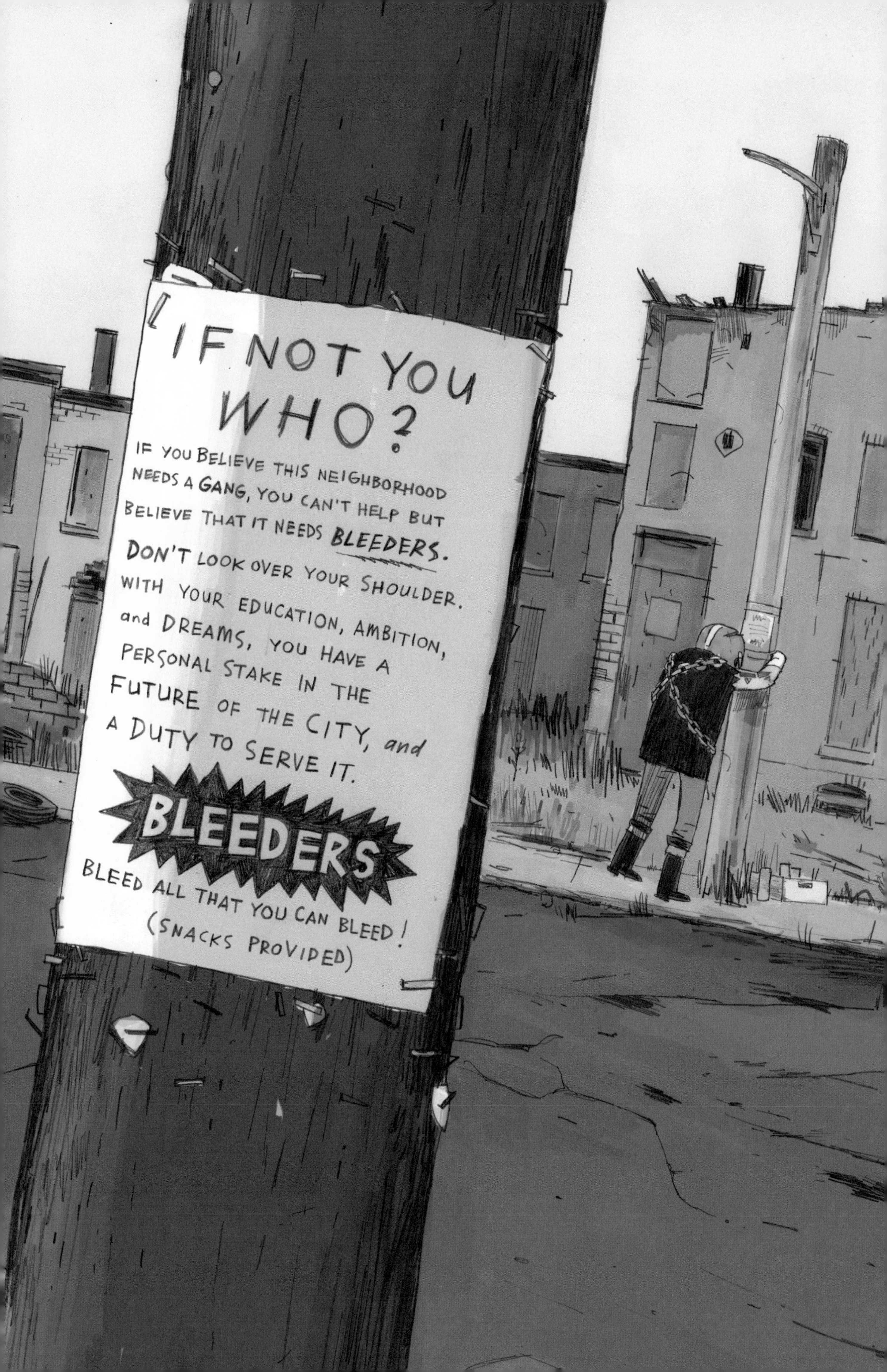
IF NOT YOU WHO?
IF YOU BELIEVE THIS NEIGHBORHOOD NEEDS A GANG, YOU CAN'T HELP BUT BELIEVE THAT IT NEEDS BLEEDERS.
DON'T LOOK OVER YOUR SHOULDER. WITH YOUR EDUCATION, AMBITION, and DREAMS, YOU HAVE A PERSONAL STAKE IN THE FUTURE OF THE CITY, and A DUTY TO SERVE IT.
BLEEDERS
BLEED ALL THAT YOU CAN BLEED!
(SNACKS PROVIDED)

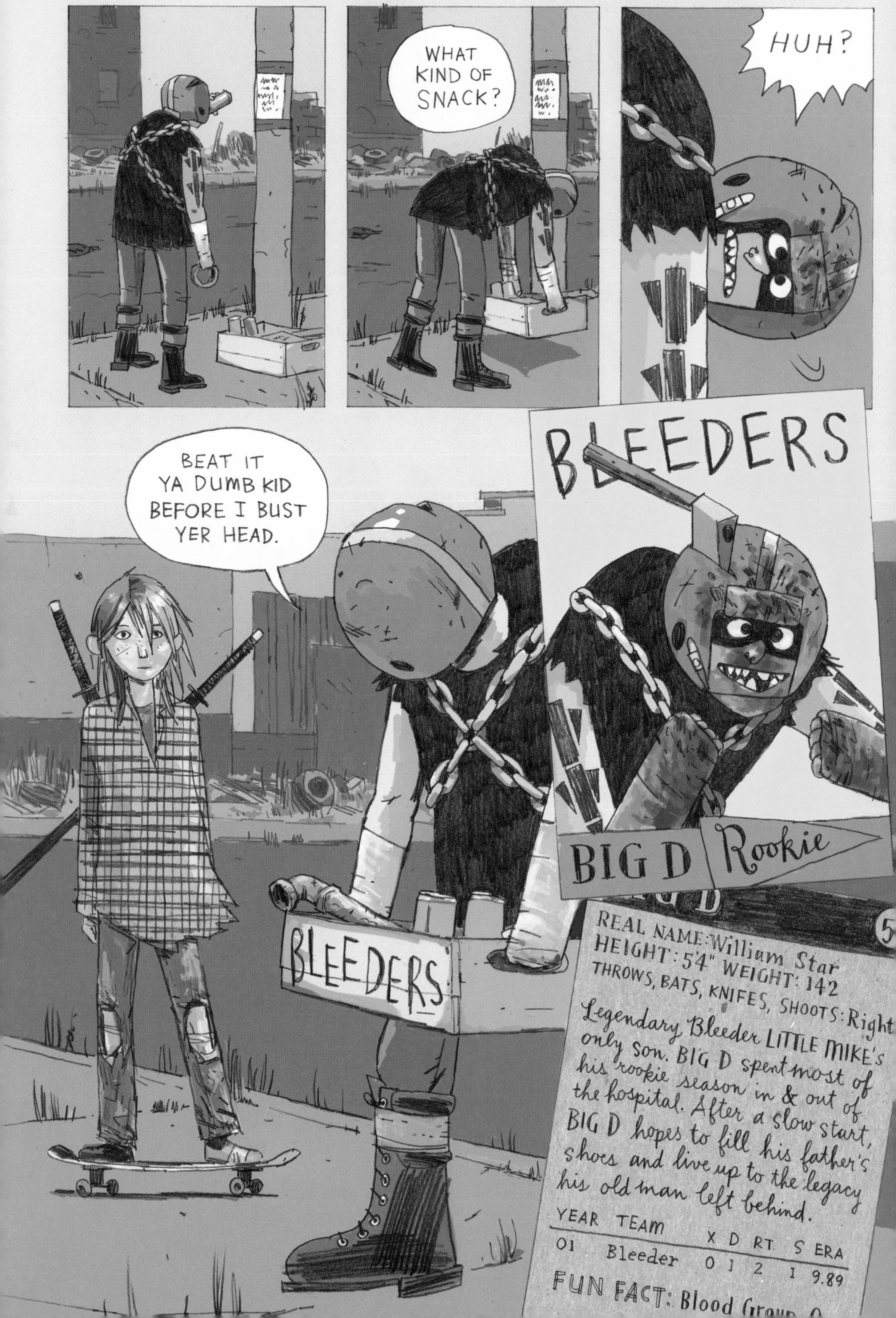
WHAT KIND OF SNACK?
HUH?
BEAT IT YA DUMB KID BEFORE I BUST YER HEAD.
BLEEDERS
BLEEDERS
BIG D
Rookie
5
REAL NAME: William Star
HEIGHT: 5'4" WEIGHT: 142
THROWS, BATS, KNIFES, SHOOTS: Right
Legendary Bleeder LITTLE MIKE's only son. BIG D spent most of his rookie season in & out of the hospital. After a slow start, BIG D hopes to fill his father's shoes and live up to the legacy his old man left behind.
YEAR TEAM X D RT. S ERA
01 Bleeder 0 1 2 1 9.89
FUN FACT: Blood

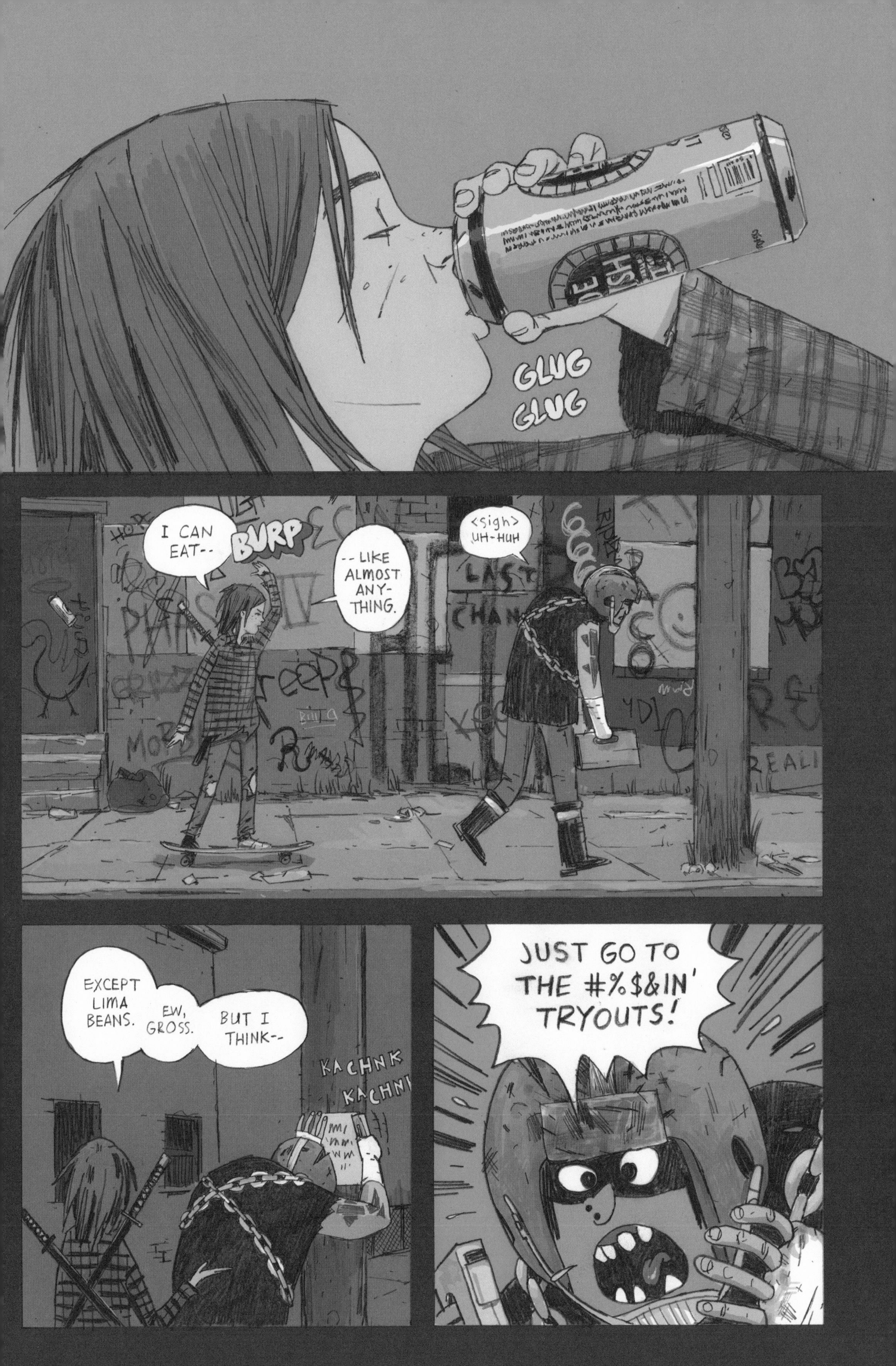
GLUG
GLUG
I CAN EAT--
BURP
--LIKE ALMOST ANY-THING.
<sigh> UH-HUH
EXCEPT LIMA BEANS.
EW, GROSS.
BUT I THINK--
KACHNK
KACHNK
JUST GO TO THE #%$&IN' TRYOUTS!

THE
STREET

ANGEL
GANG

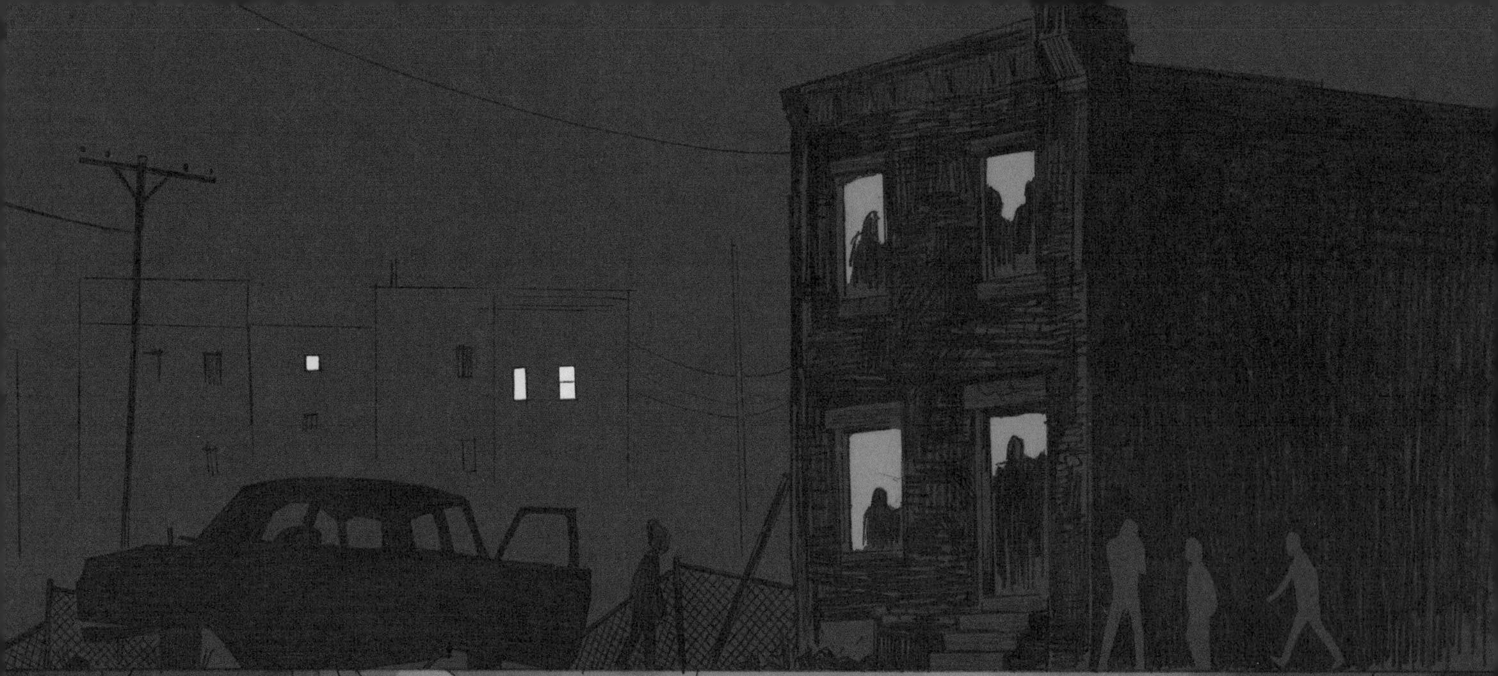

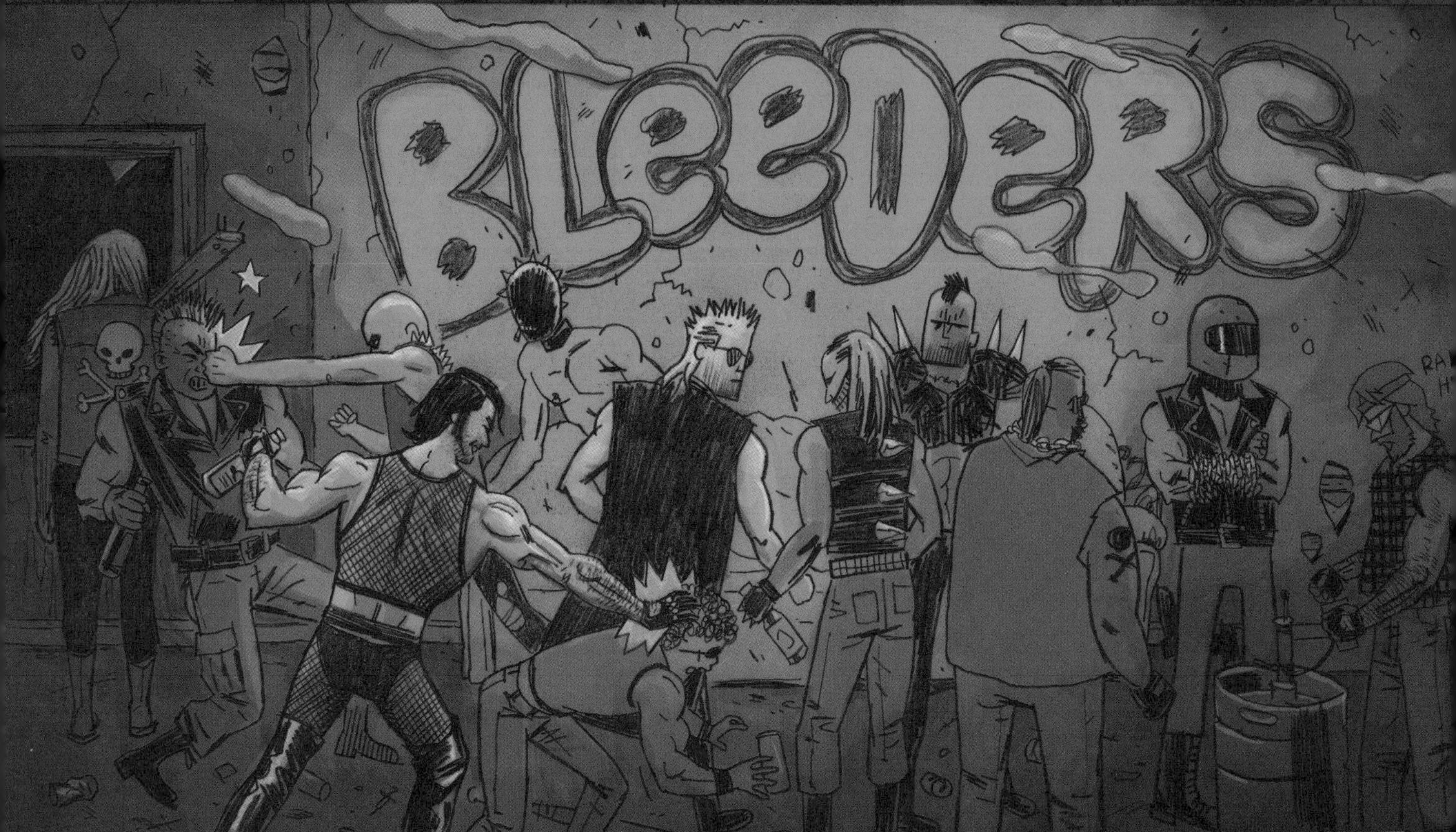
BLEEDERS

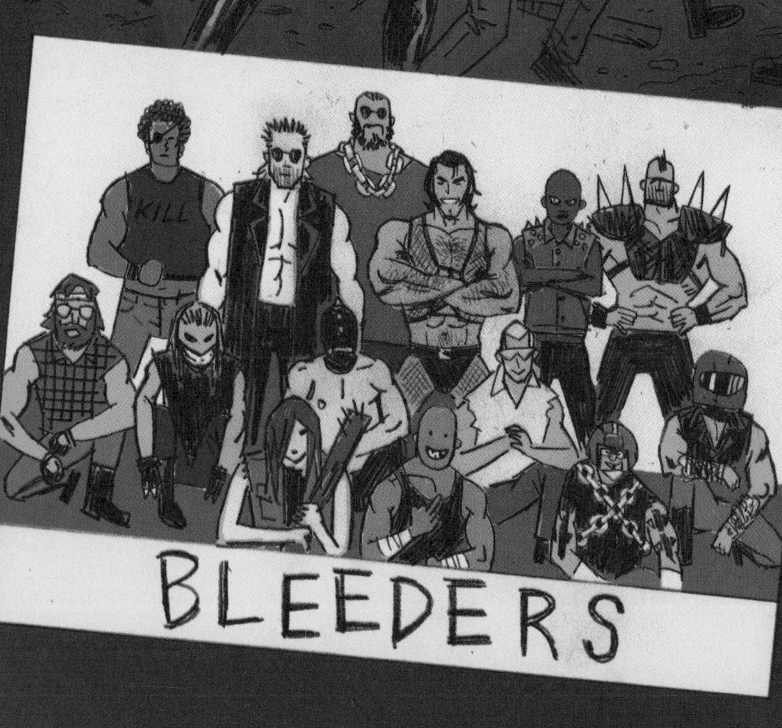
KILL
BLEEDERS

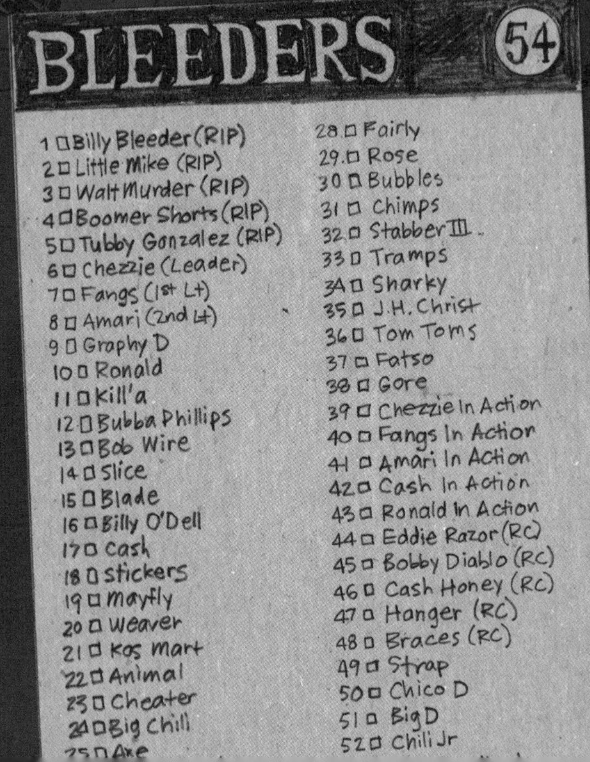
BLEEDERS
54
1 □ Billy Bleeder (RIP)
2 □ Little Mike (RIP)
3 □ Walt Murder (RIP)
4 □ Boomer Shorts (RIP)
5 □ Tubby Gonzalez (RIP)
6 □ Chezzie (Leader)
7 □ Fangs (1st Lt)
8 □ Amari (2nd Lt)
9 □ Graphy D
10 □ Ronald
11 □ Kill'a
12 □ Bubba Phillips
13 □ Bob Wire
14 □ Slice
15 □ Blade
16 □ Billy O'Dell
17 □ Cash
18 □ Stickers
19 □ Mayfly
20 □ Weaver
21 □ Kos Mart
22 □ Animal
23 □ Cheater
24 □ Big Chill
25 □ Axe
28 □ Fairly
29. □ Rose
30 □ Bubbles
31 □ Chimps
32 □ Stabber III
33 □ Tramps
34 □ Sharky
35 □ J.H. Christ
36 □ Tom Toms
37 □ Fatso
38 □ Gore
39 □ Chezzie In Action
40 □ Fangs In Action
41 □ Amari In Action
42 □ Cash In Action
43 □ Ronald In Action
44 □ Eddie Razor (RC)
45 □ Bobby Diablo (RC)
46 □ Cash Honey (RC)
47 □ Hanger (RC)
48 □ Braces (RC)
49 □ Strap
50 □ Chico D
51 □ Big D
52 □ Chili Jr

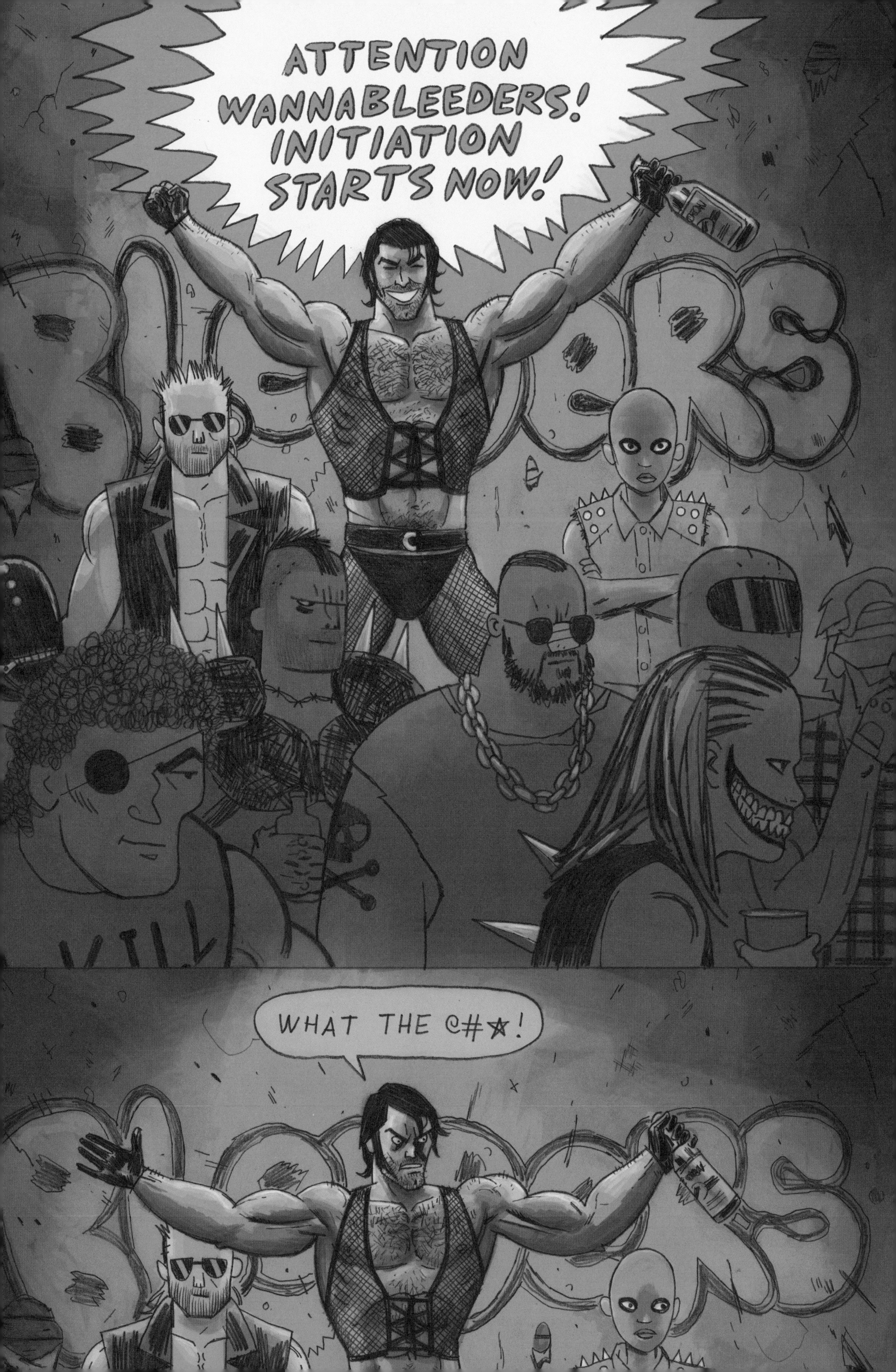
ATTENTION WANNABLEEDERS! INITIATION STARTS NOW!
WHAT THE C#☆!

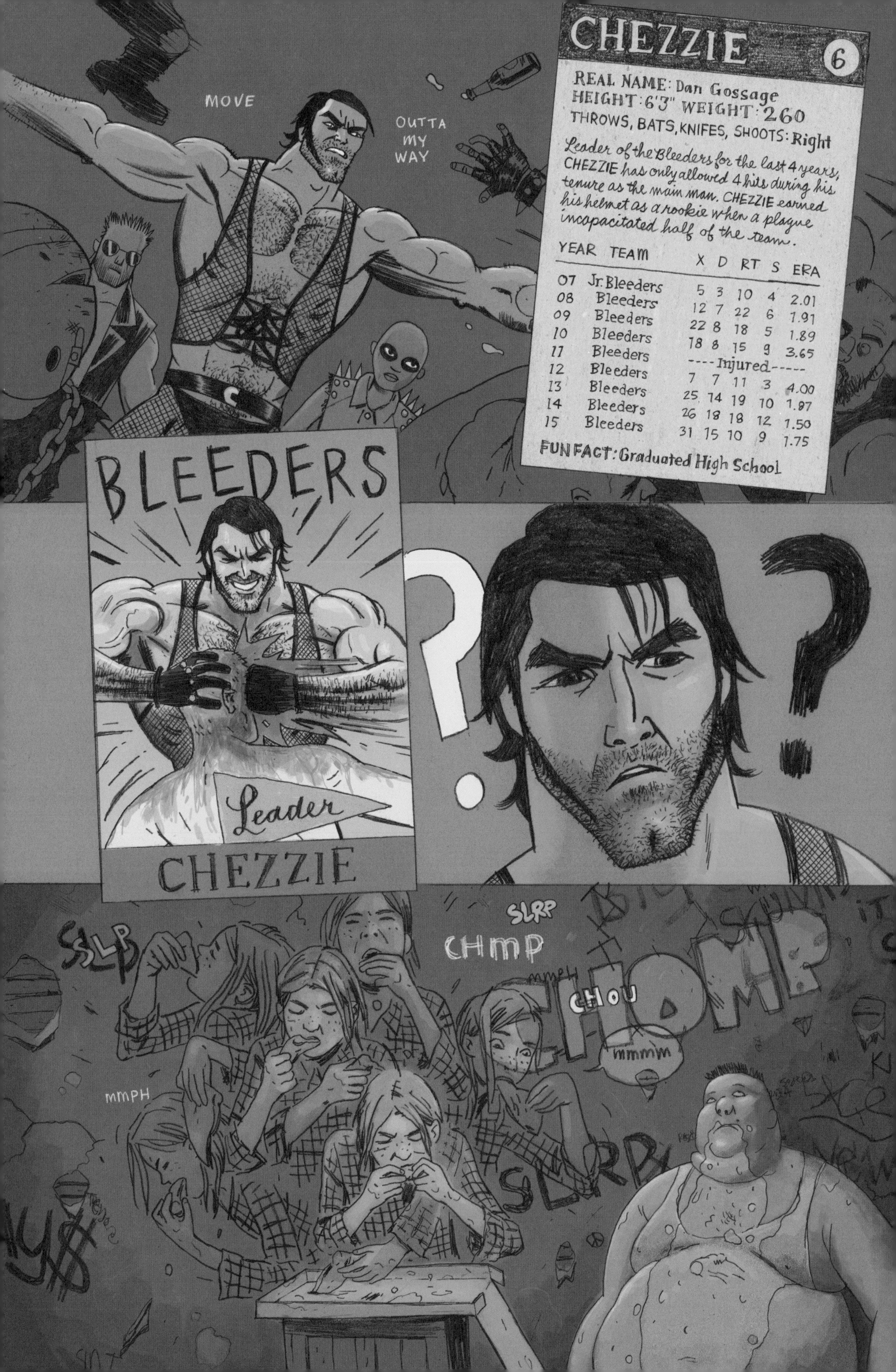
MOVE
OUTTA MY WAY
CHEZZIE
6
REAL NAME: Dan Gossage
HEIGHT: 6'3" WEIGHT: 260
THROWS, BATS, KNIFES, SHOOTS: Right
Leader of the Bleeders for the last 4 years, CHEZZIE has only allowed 4 hits during his tenure as the main man. CHEZZIE earned his helmet as a rookie when a plague incapacitated half of the team.
YEAR TEAM X D RT S ERA
07 Jr. Bleeders 5 3 10 4 2.01
08 Bleeders 12 7 22 6 1.91
09 Bleeders 22 8 18 5 1.89
10 Bleeders 18 8 15 9 3.65
11 Bleeders ----Injured-----
12 Bleeders 7 7 11 3 4.00
13 Bleeders 25 14 19 10 1.87
14 Bleeders 26 18 18 12 1.50
15 Bleeders 31 15 10 9 1.75
FUN FACT: Graduated High School
BLEEDERS
Leader
CHEZZIE
?
?
!
SLP
SLRP
CHMP
mmph
CHOU
CHOMP
mmmm
MMPH
SLRP

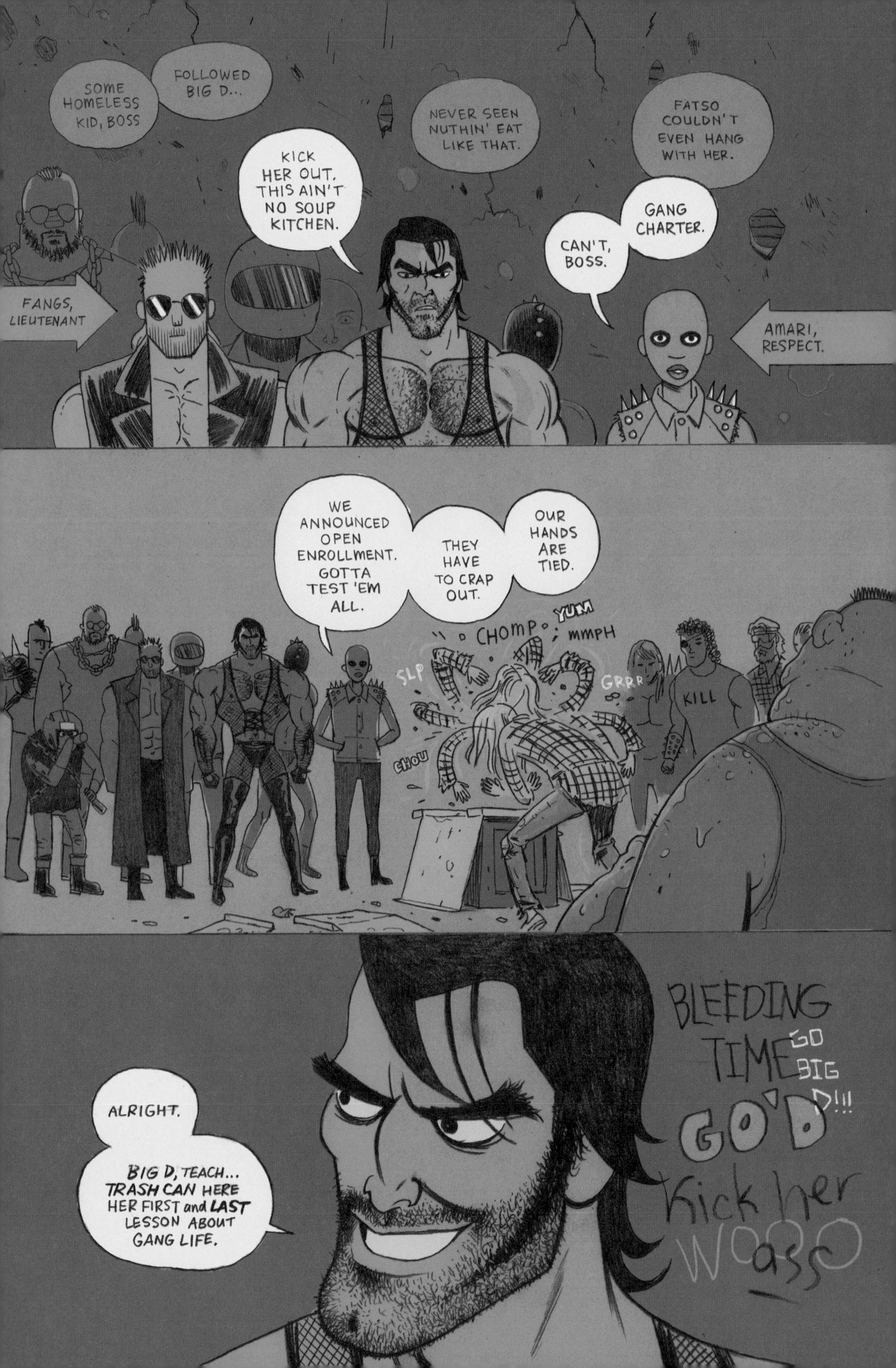
SOME HOMELESS KID, BOSS
FOLLOWED BIG D...
KICK HER OUT. THIS AIN'T NO SOUP KITCHEN.
NEVER SEEN NUTHIN' EAT LIKE THAT.
FATSO COULDN'T EVEN HANG WITH HER.
CAN'T, BOSS.
GANG CHARTER.
FANGS, LIEUTENANT
AMARI, RESPECT.
WE ANNOUNCED OPEN ENROLLMENT. GOTTA TEST 'EM ALL.
THEY HAVE TO CRAP OUT.
OUR HANDS ARE TIED.
CHOMP
YUM
mmpH
SLP
GRRR
CHOU
KILL
ALRIGHT.
BIG D, TEACH... TRASH CAN HERE HER FIRST and LAST LESSON ABOUT GANG LIFE.
BLEEDING TIME
GO BIG D!!!
GO'D
Kick her ass
WOOO

GANG RULE #1: 9#★! ROLLS DOWN HILL.

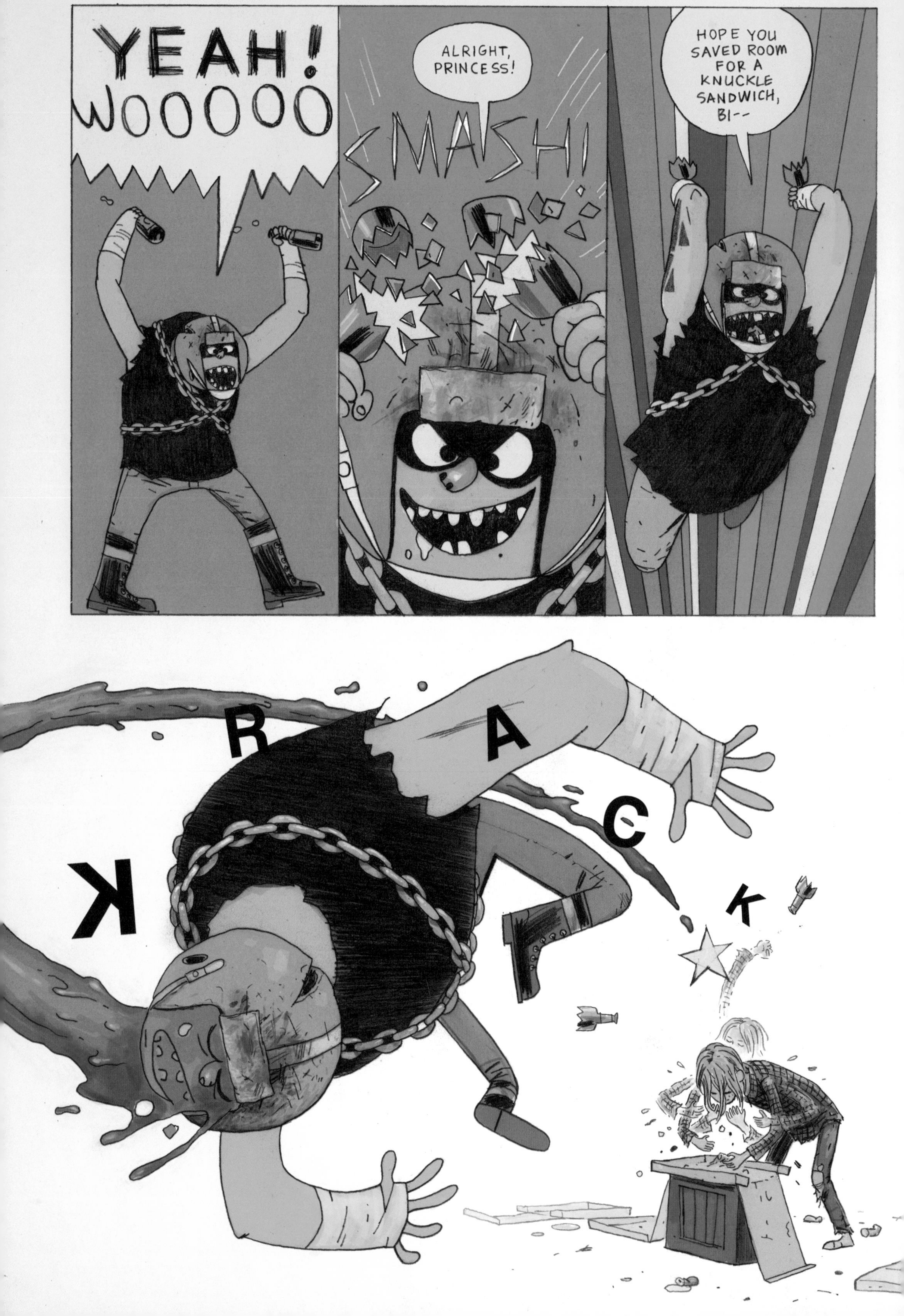
YEAH! WOOOOO
ALRIGHT, PRINCESS!
SMASH!
HOPE YOU SAVED ROOM FOR A KNUCKLE SANDWICH, BI--
KRACK

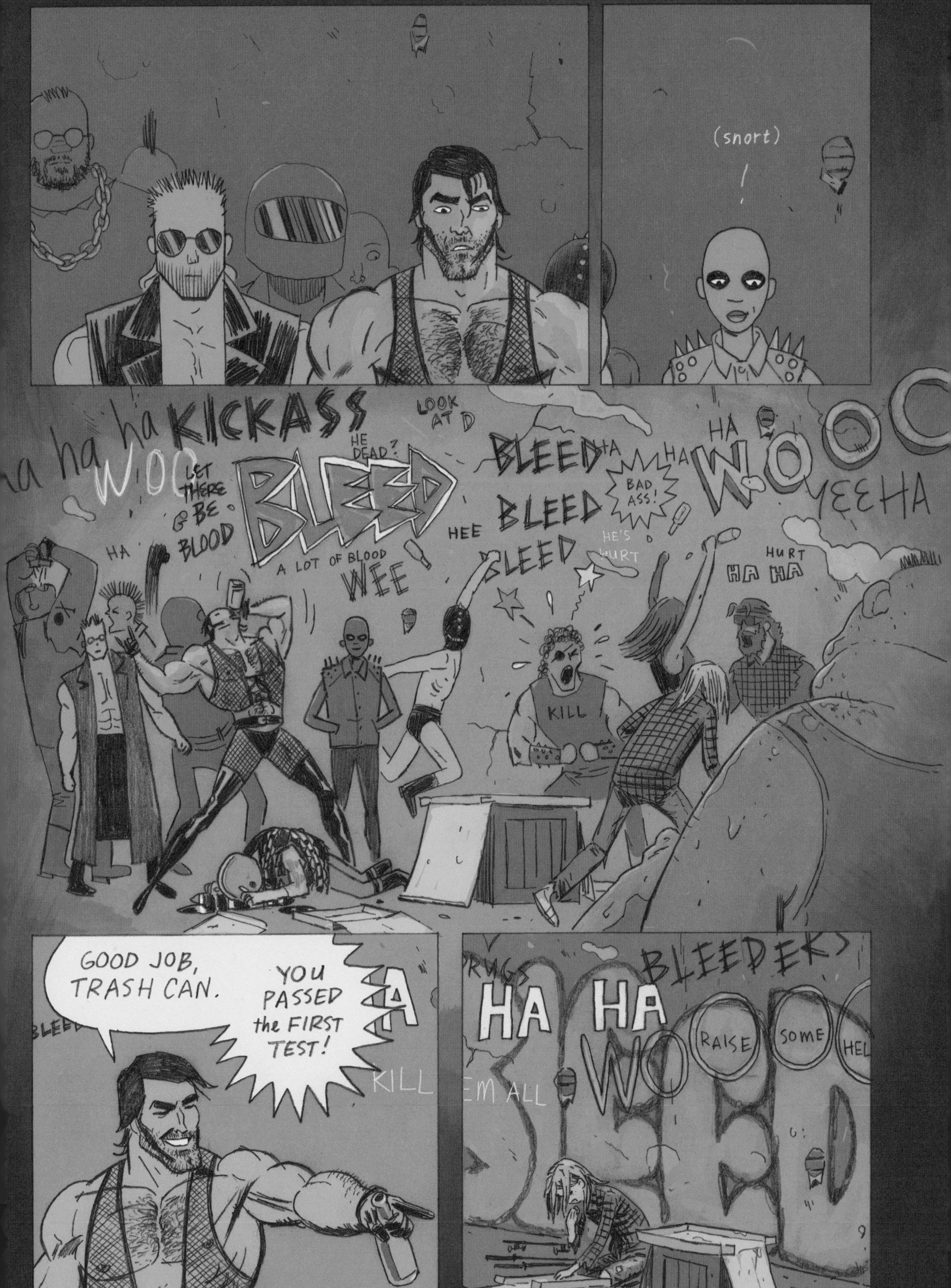

(snort)
ha ha ha KICKASS
WOO
LOOK AT D
HE DEAD?
LET THERE BE BLOOD
BLEED
A LOT OF BLOOD
WEE
HA
HEE
BLEED HA
BLEED
BLEED
BAD ASS!
HE'S HURT
HA HA WOOO
YEEHA
HURT
HA HA
KILL
GOOD JOB, TRASH CAN.
YOU PASSED the FIRST TEST!
BLEED
A
KILL EM ALL
DRUGS
BLEEDERS
HA HA
WOO
RAISE
SOME
HEL
BLEED

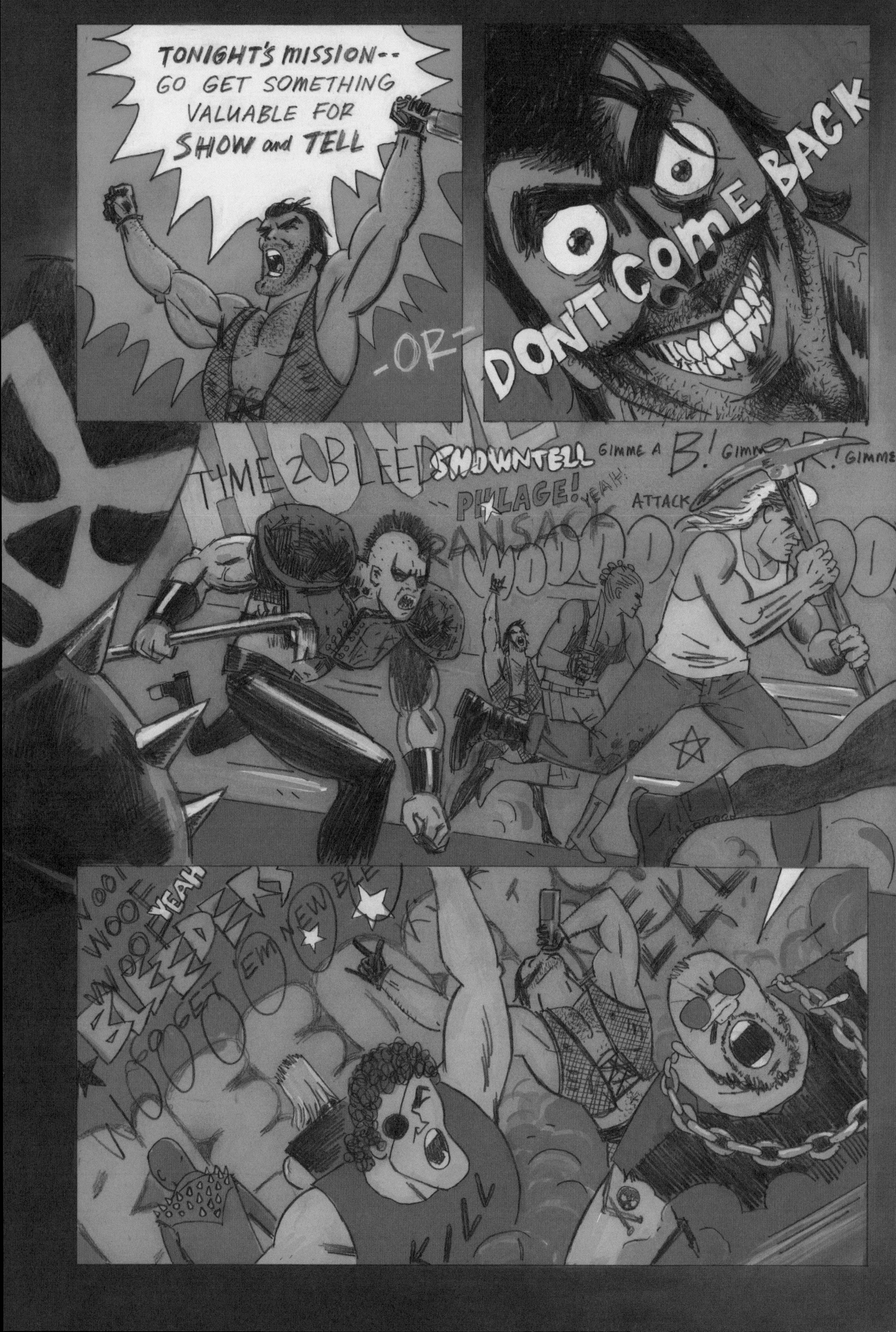
TONIGHT'S MISSION-- GO GET SOMETHING VALUABLE FOR SHOW and TELL
-OR-
DON'T COME BACK
TIME 2 BLEED
SHOWNTELL
GIMME A B! GIMME
PILLAGE!
YEAH!
ATTACK
RANSACK
YEAH
'EM NEW

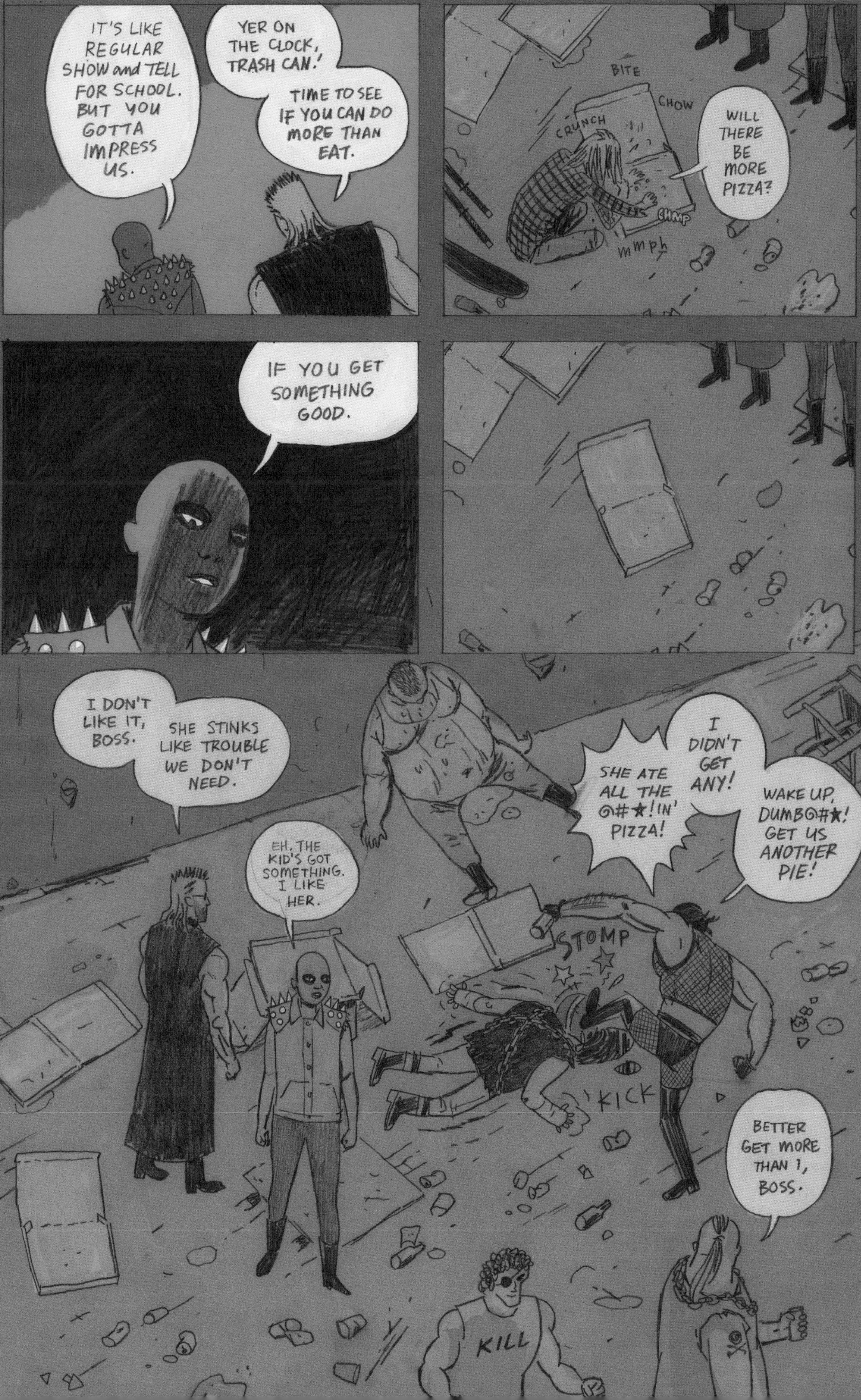
IT'S LIKE REGULAR SHOW and TELL FOR SCHOOL. BUT YOU GOTTA IMPRESS US.
YER ON THE CLOCK, TRASH CAN.
TIME TO SEE IF YOU CAN DO MORE THAN EAT.
BITE
CHOW
CRUNCH
WILL THERE BE MORE PIZZA?
CHMP
mmph
IF YOU GET SOMETHING GOOD.
I DON'T LIKE IT, BOSS.
SHE STINKS LIKE TROUBLE WE DON'T NEED.
EH, THE KID'S GOT SOMETHING. I LIKE HER.
SHE ATE ALL THE @#★!IN' PIZZA!
I DIDN'T GET ANY!
WAKE UP, DUMB@#★! GET US ANOTHER PIE!
STOMP
KICK
BETTER GET MORE THAN 1, BOSS.
KILL

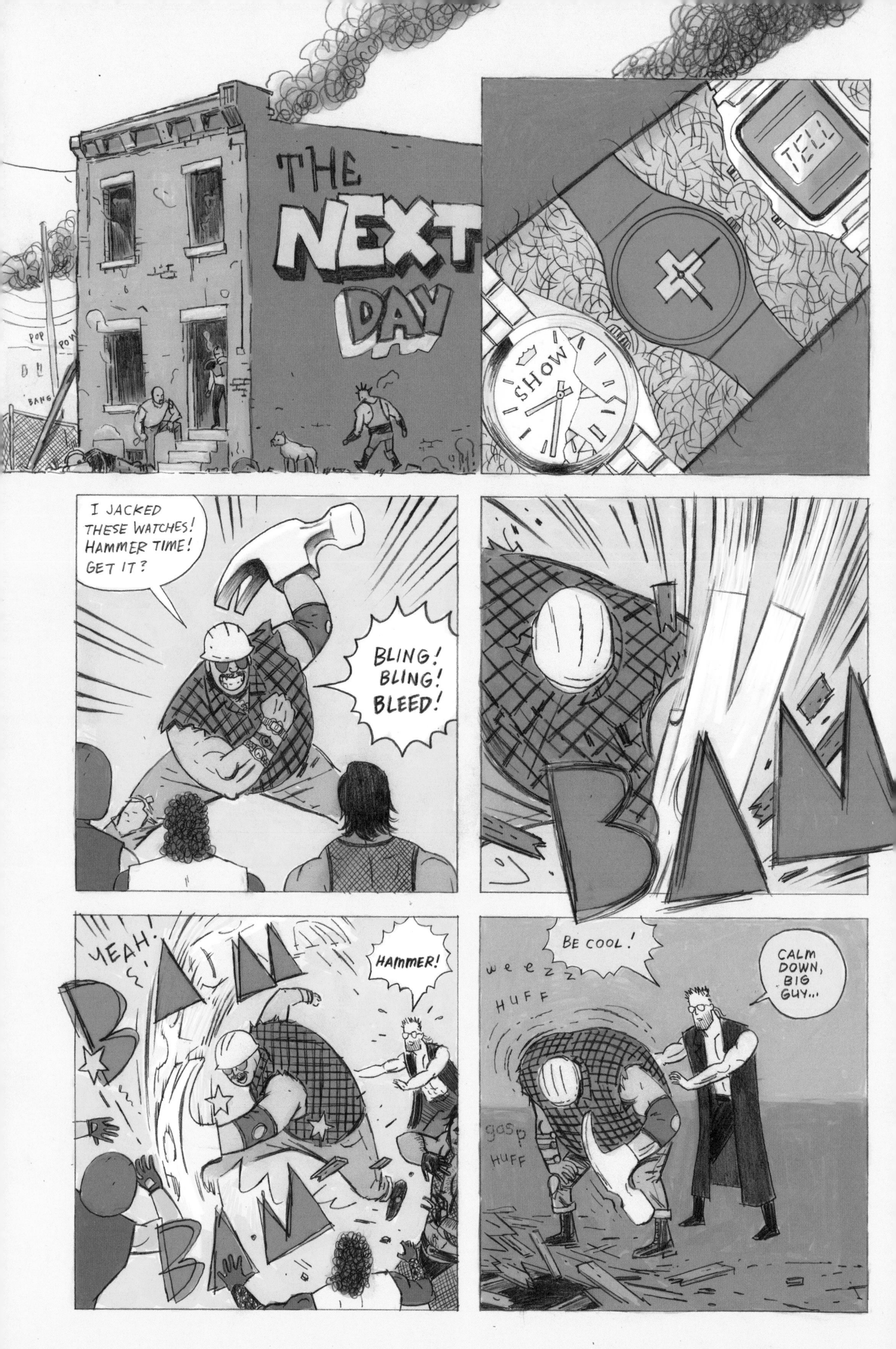
THE NEXT DAY
POP
POW
BANG
TELL
SHOW
I JACKED THESE WATCHES! HAMMER TIME! GET IT?
BLING! BLING! BLEED!
BAM
YEAH!
BAM
HAMMER!
BAM
BE COOL!
weezz
HUFF
CALM DOWN, BIG GUY...
gasp
HUFF

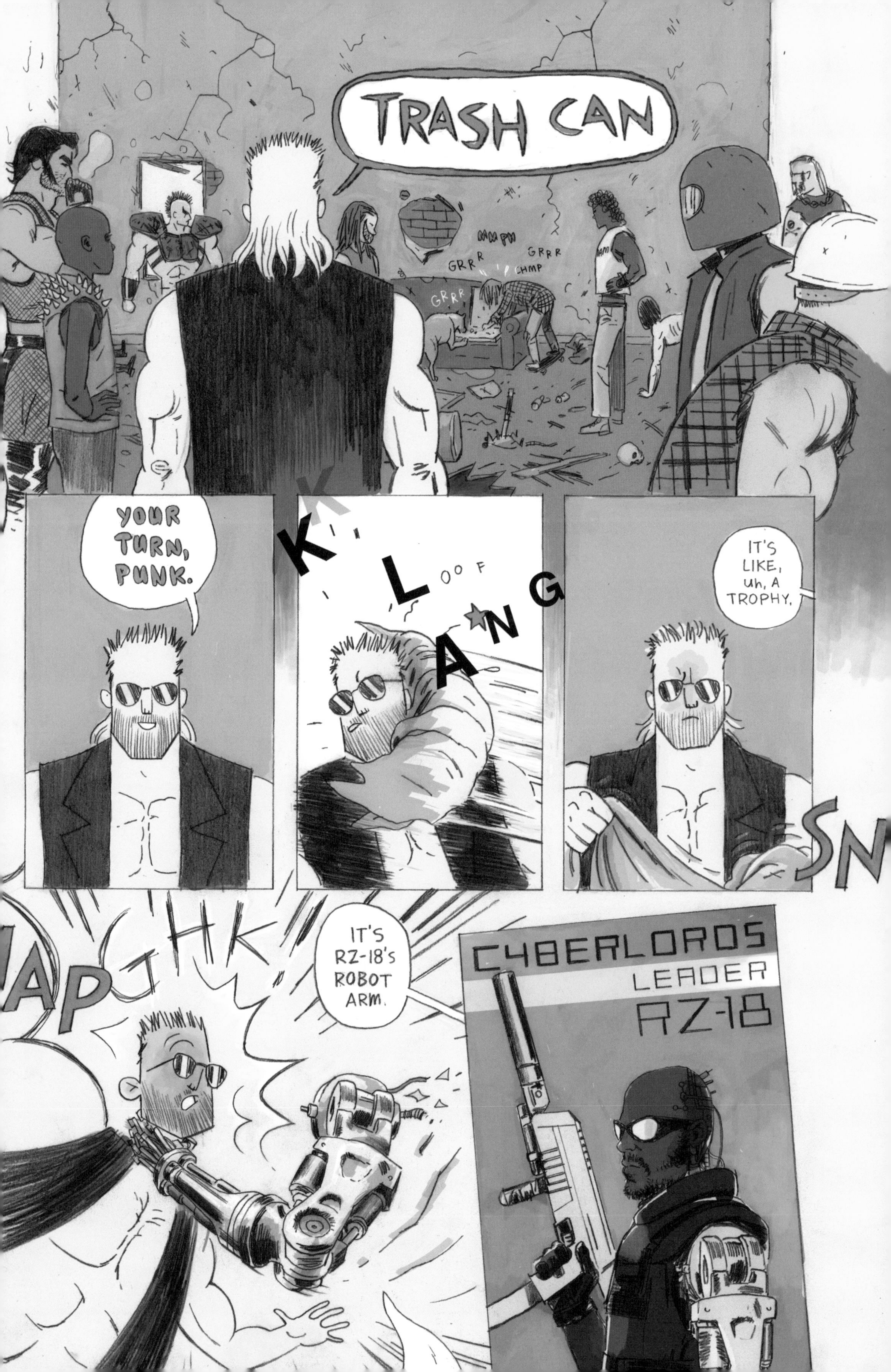
TRASH CAN
MMPH
GRRR
GRRR
CHMP
GRRR
YOUR TURN, PUNK.
KLANG
OOF
IT'S LIKE, uh, A TROPHY.
SN
AP
THK
IT'S RZ-18's ROBOT ARM.
CYBERLORDS LEADER
RZ-18

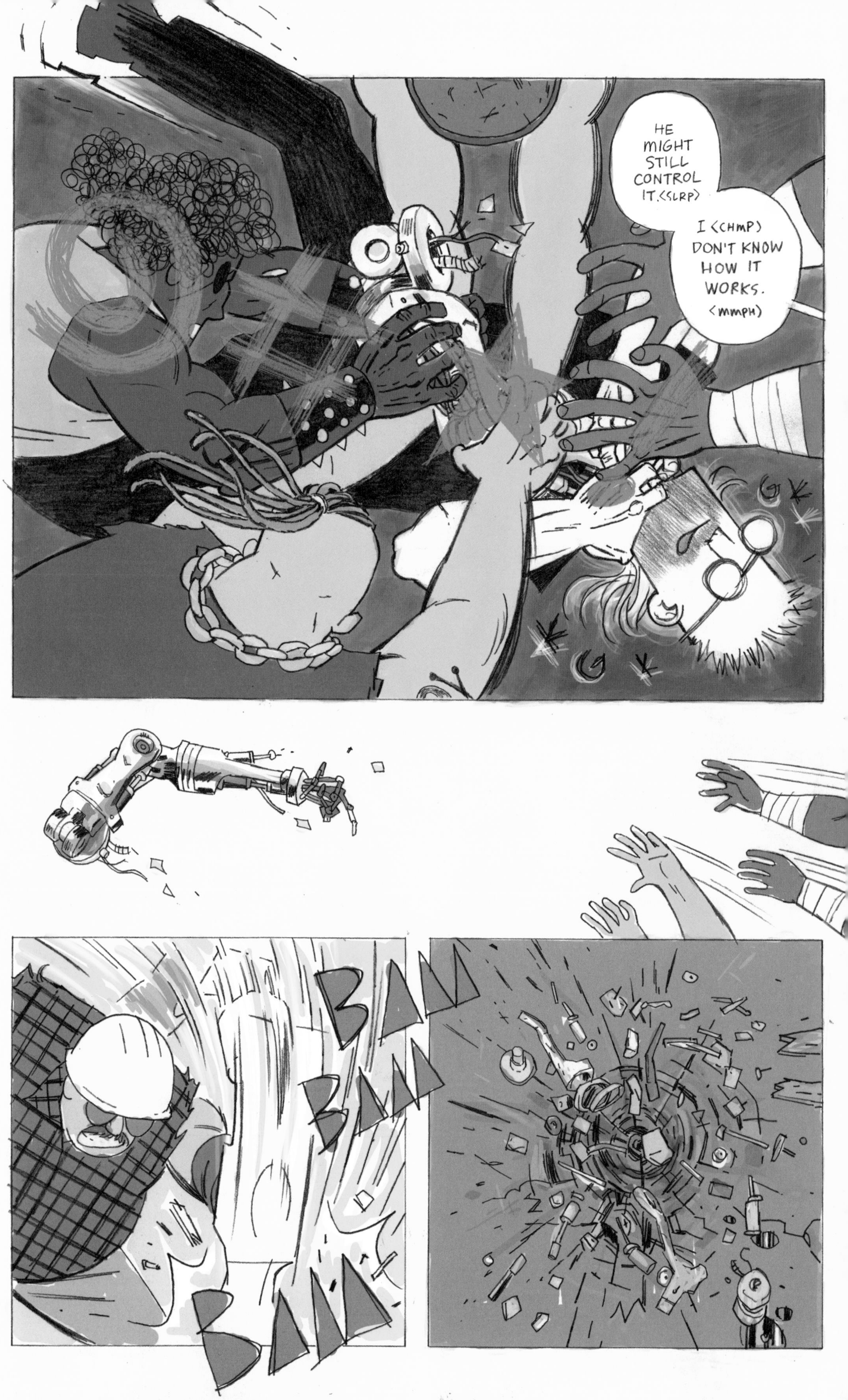
HE MIGHT STILL CONTROL IT. <SLRP>
I <CHMP> DON'T KNOW HOW IT WORKS. <MMPH>

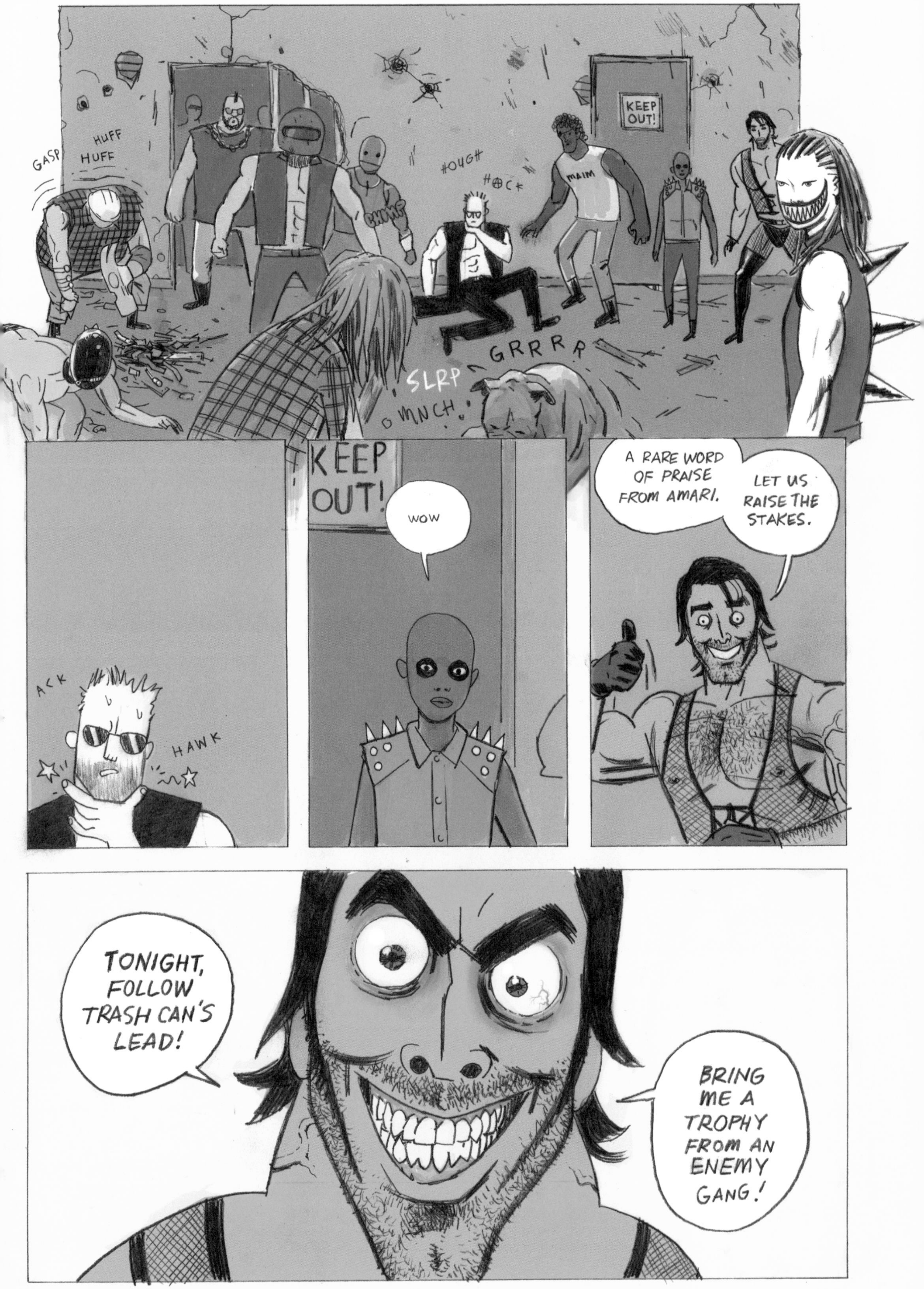
GASP
HUFF
HUFF
KEEP OUT!
HOUGH
HACK
MAIM
GRRRR
SLRP
MNCH
ACK
HAWK
KEEP OUT!
WOW
A RARE WORD OF PRAISE FROM AMARI.
LET US RAISE THE STAKES.
TONIGHT, FOLLOW TRASH CAN'S LEAD!
BRING ME A TROPHY FROM AN ENEMY GANG!

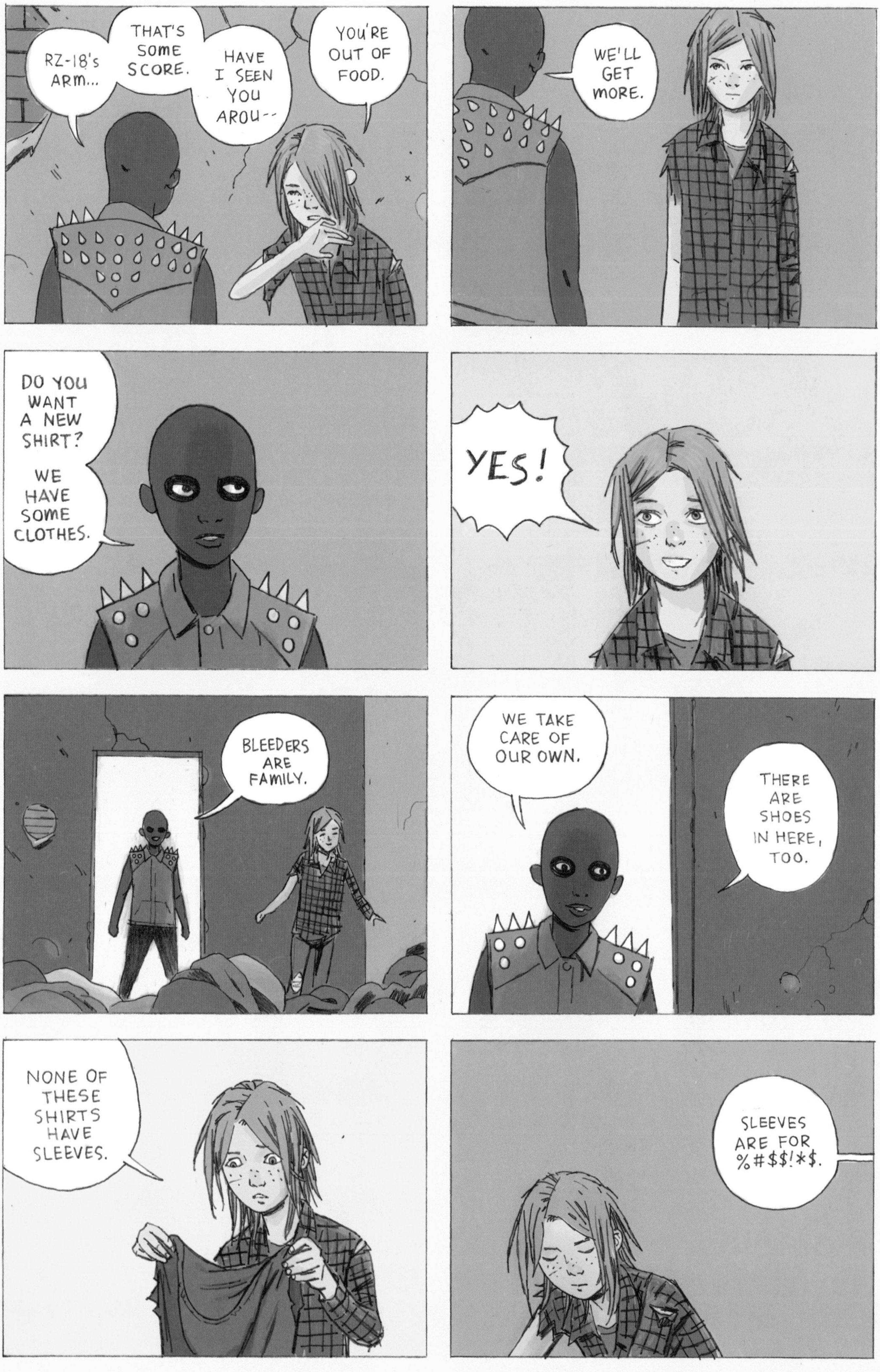
RZ-18's ARM...
THAT'S SOME SCORE.
HAVE I SEEN YOU AROU--
YOU'RE OUT OF FOOD.
WE'LL GET MORE.
DO YOU WANT A NEW SHIRT?
WE HAVE SOME CLOTHES.
YES!
BLEEDERS ARE FAMILY.
WE TAKE CARE OF OUR OWN.
THERE ARE SHOES IN HERE, TOO.
NONE OF THESE SHIRTS HAVE SLEEVES.
SLEEVES ARE FOR %#$$!*$.

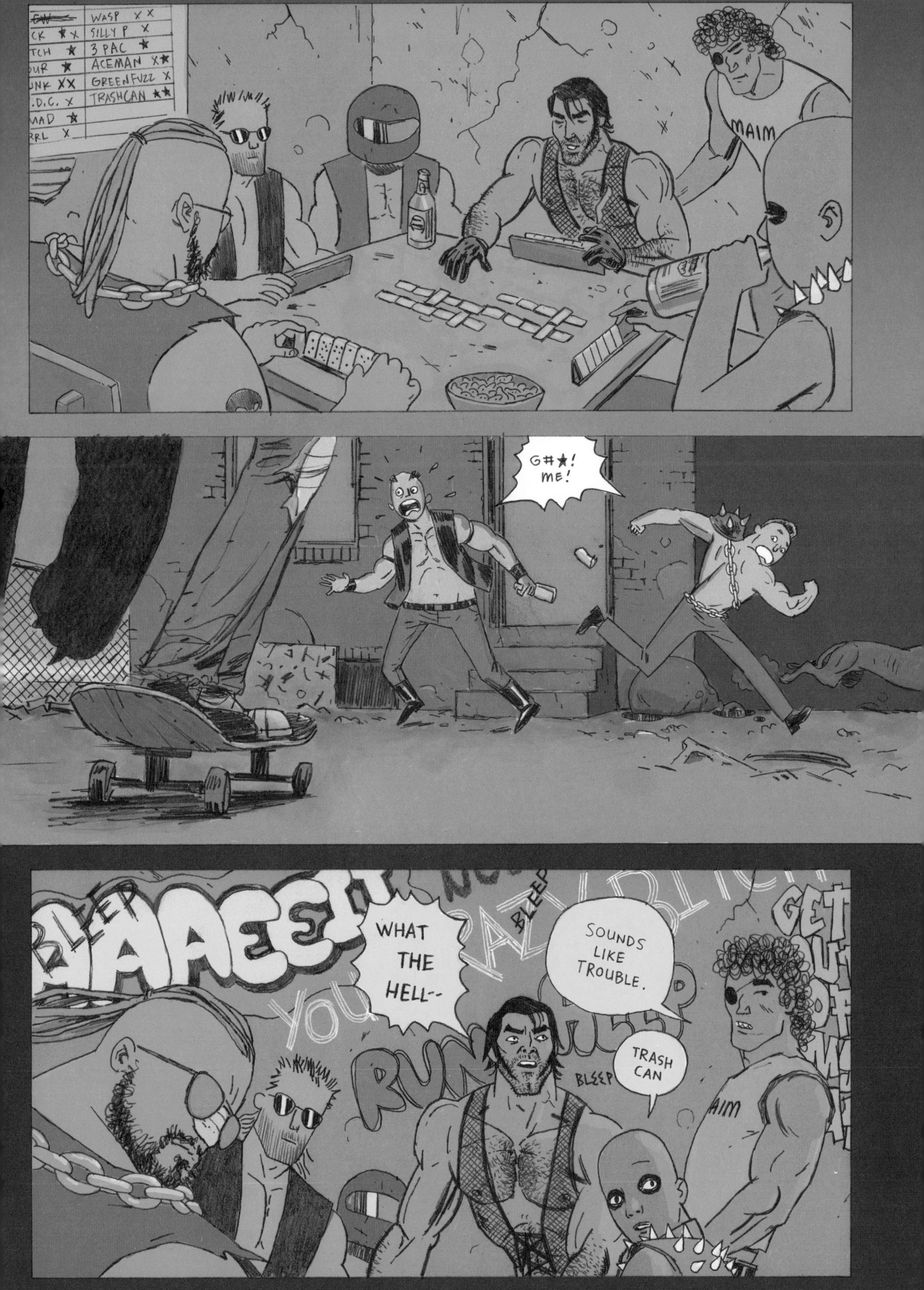
WASP X X
SILLY P X
3 PAC ★
ACEMAN X★
GREENFUZZ X
TRASHCAN ★★
MAIM
G#★! ME!
BLEEP
WHAT THE HELL--
YOU
BLEEP
SOUNDS LIKE TROUBLE.
RUN
TRASH CAN
BLEEP
GET
MAIM

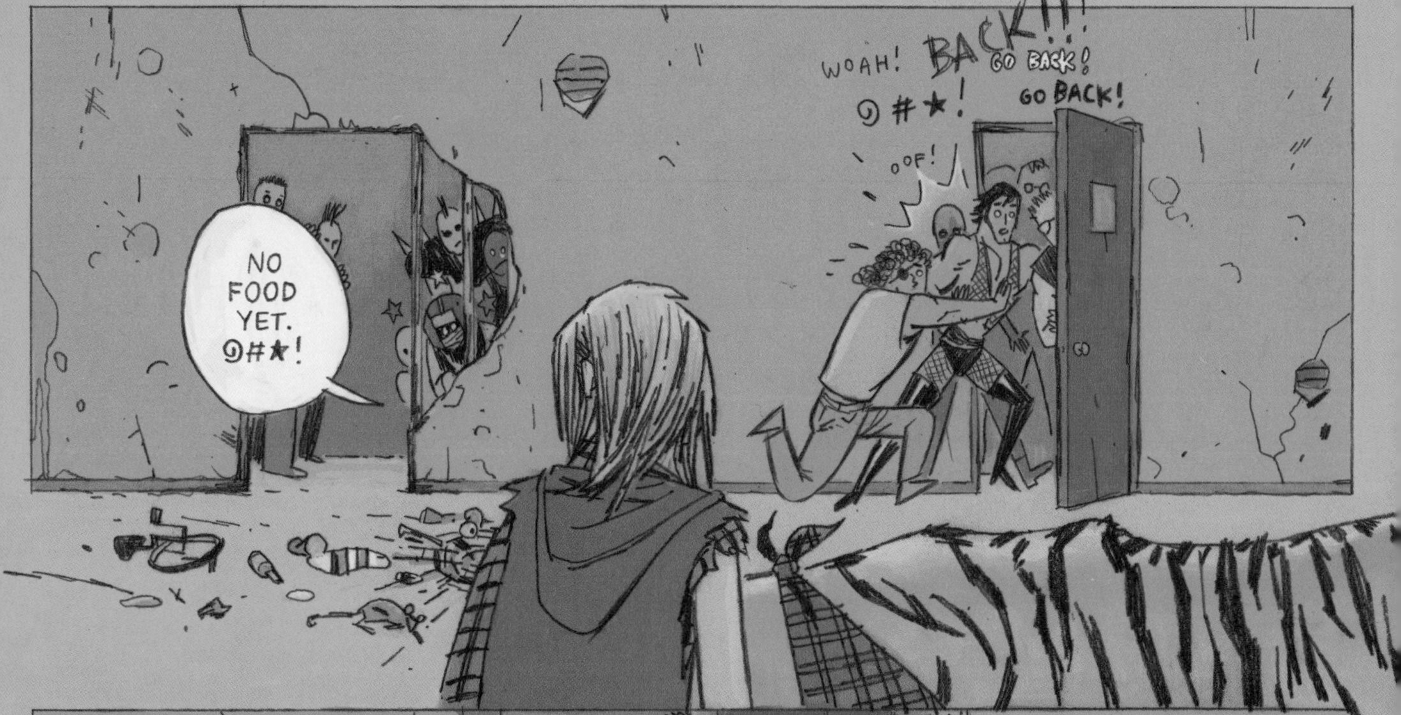
NO FOOD YET. ☉#★!
WOAH! BACK!!! GO BACK! GO BACK!
☉#★!
OOF!

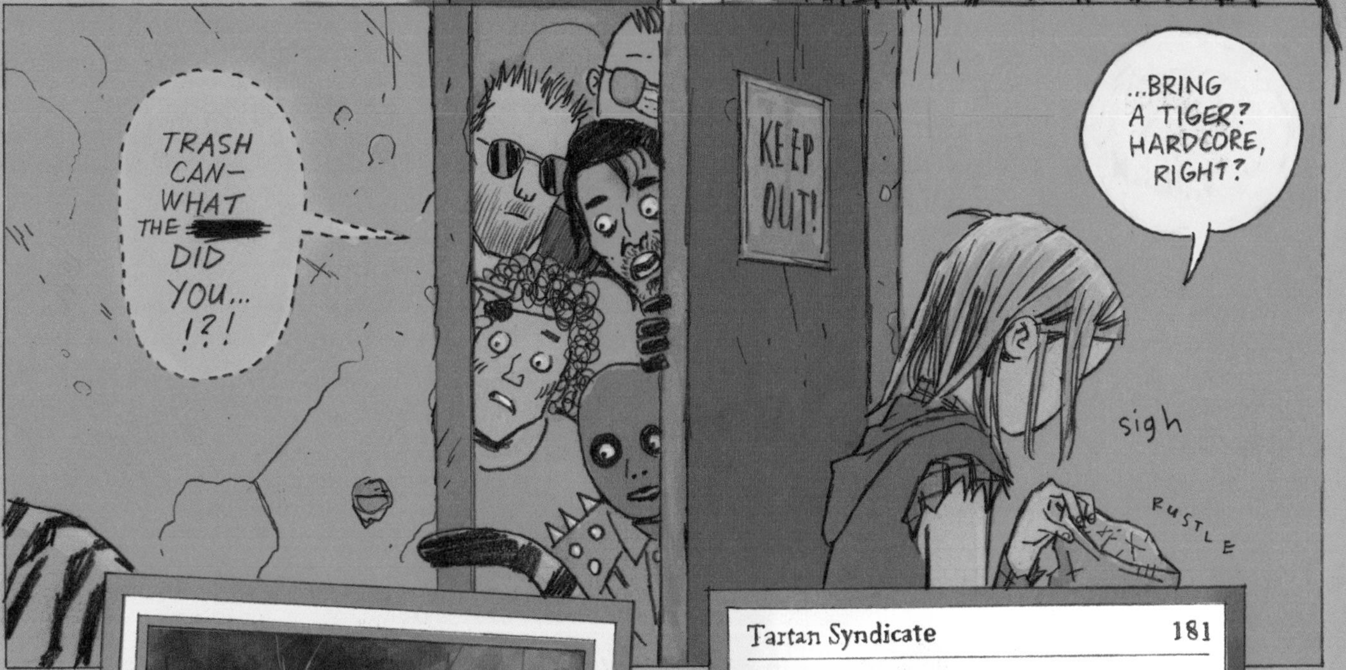
TRASH CAN— WHAT THE [redacted] DID YOU... !?!
KEEP OUT!
...BRING A TIGER? HARDCORE, RIGHT?
sigh
RUSTLE

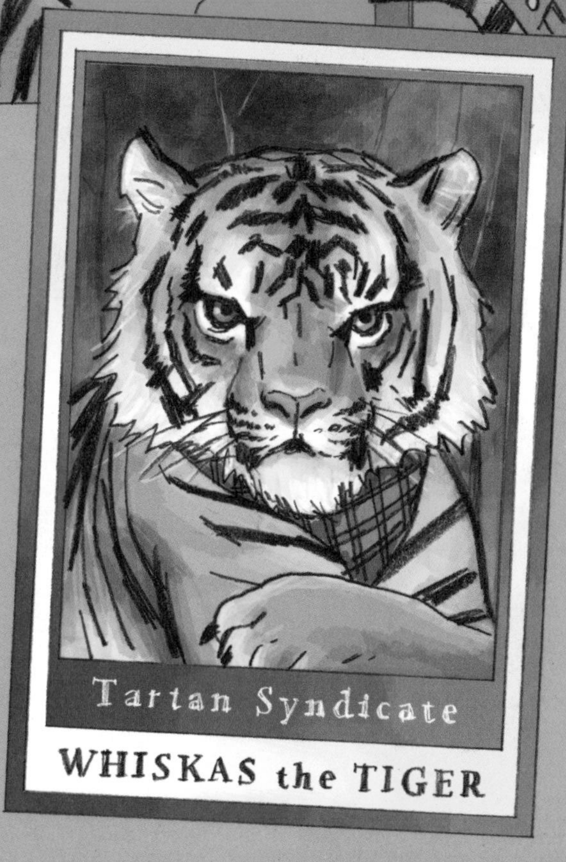
Tartan Syndicate
WHISKAS the TIGER

Tartan Syndicate 181

WHISKAS the Tiger

INTELLIGENCE
STRENGTH
SPEED
AGILITY
FIGHTING SKILL

Saved from a poacher's bulletas a kitten. Whiskas swore fealty to her rescuer, Laird Connor McDougall. Until she repays her blood-debt, McDougall's blindside is secure.

UNCONFIRMED:
She has mastery of several deadly forms of Kung Fu, including Crane, Cobra, Praying Mantis (southern style), Monkey, and Scorpion.

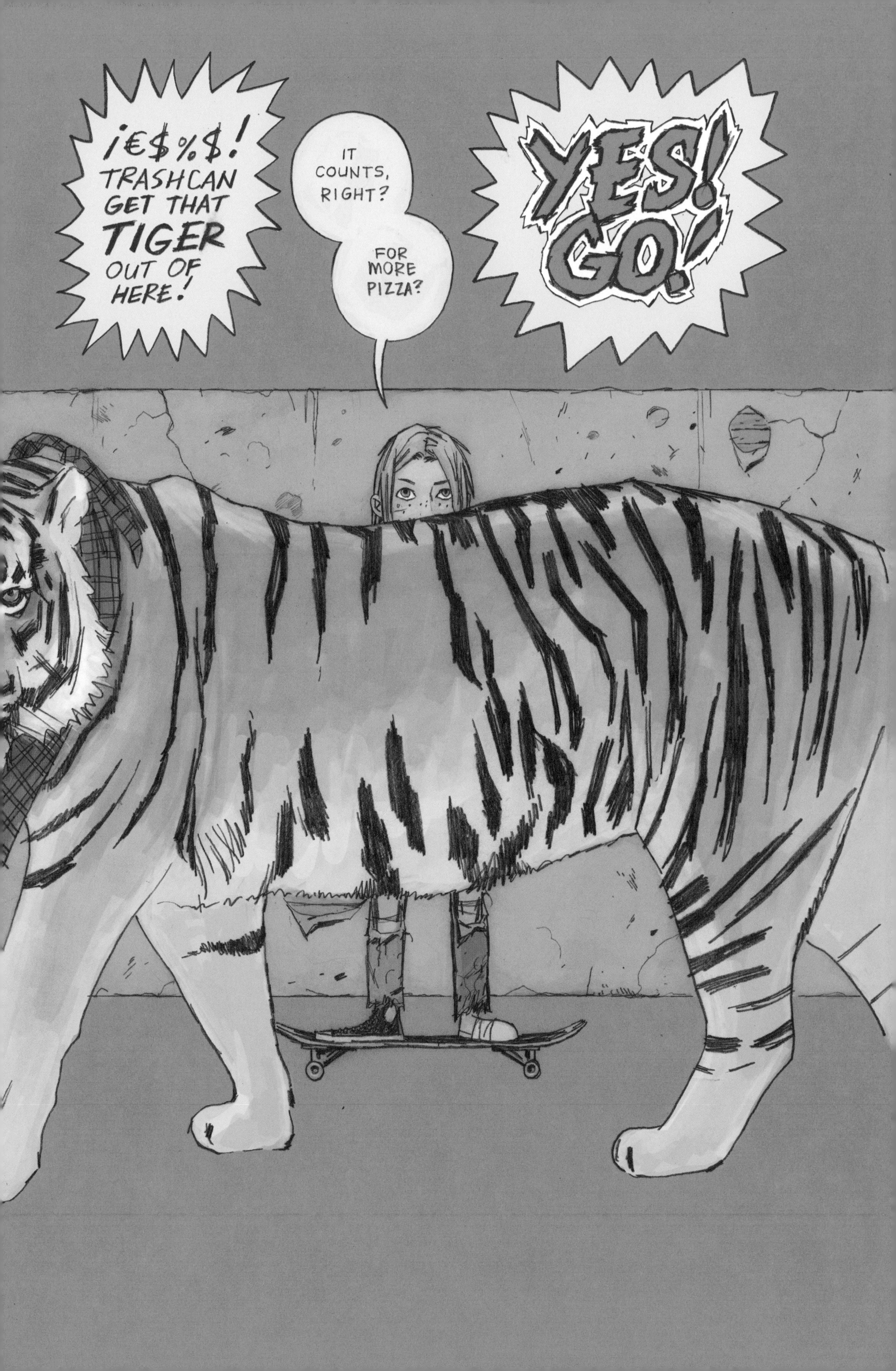
¡€$%$! TRASHCAN GET THAT TIGER OUT OF HERE!
IT COUNTS, RIGHT?
FOR MORE PIZZA?
YES! GO!

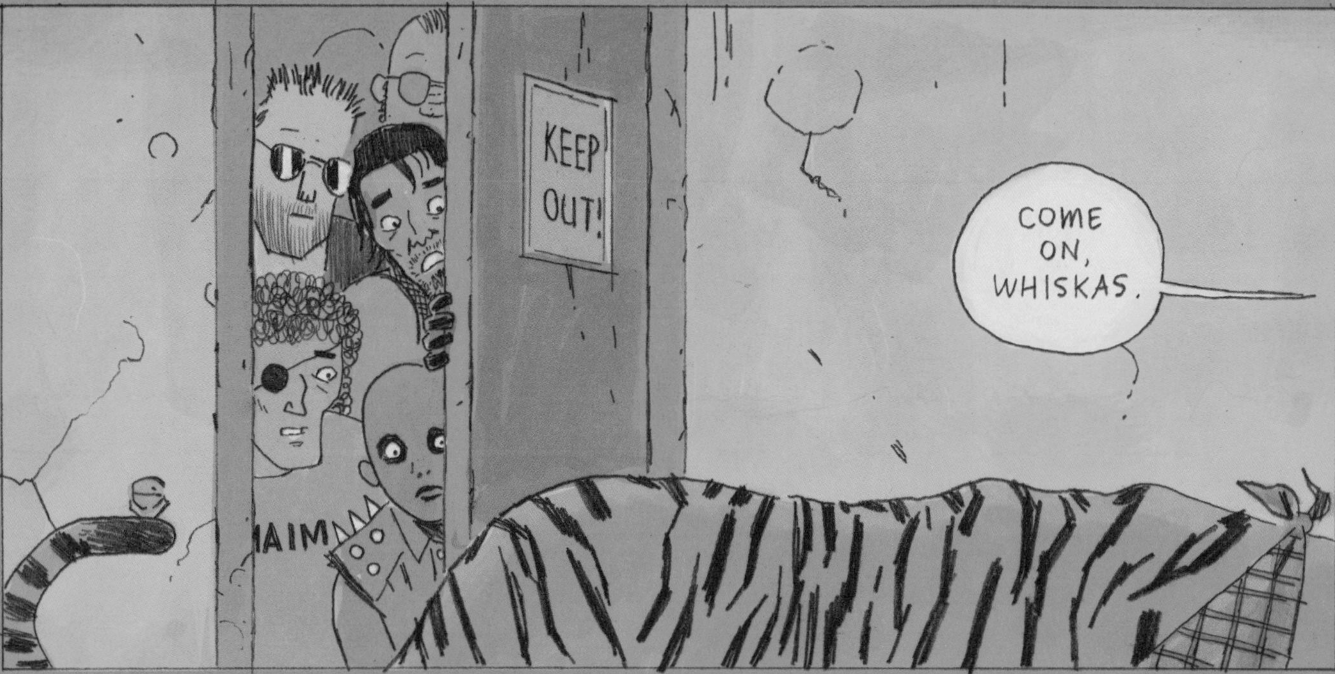
KEEP OUT!
COME ON, WHISKAS.
MAIM

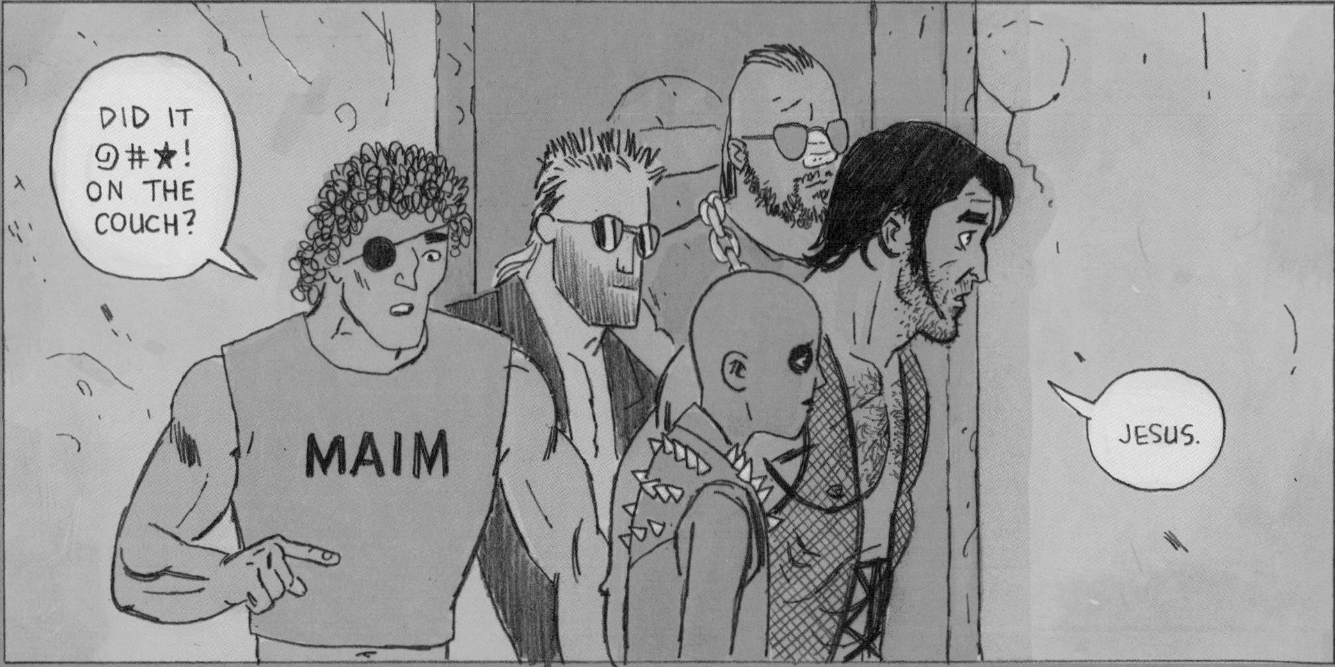
DID IT @#★! ON THE COUCH?
MAIM
JESUS.

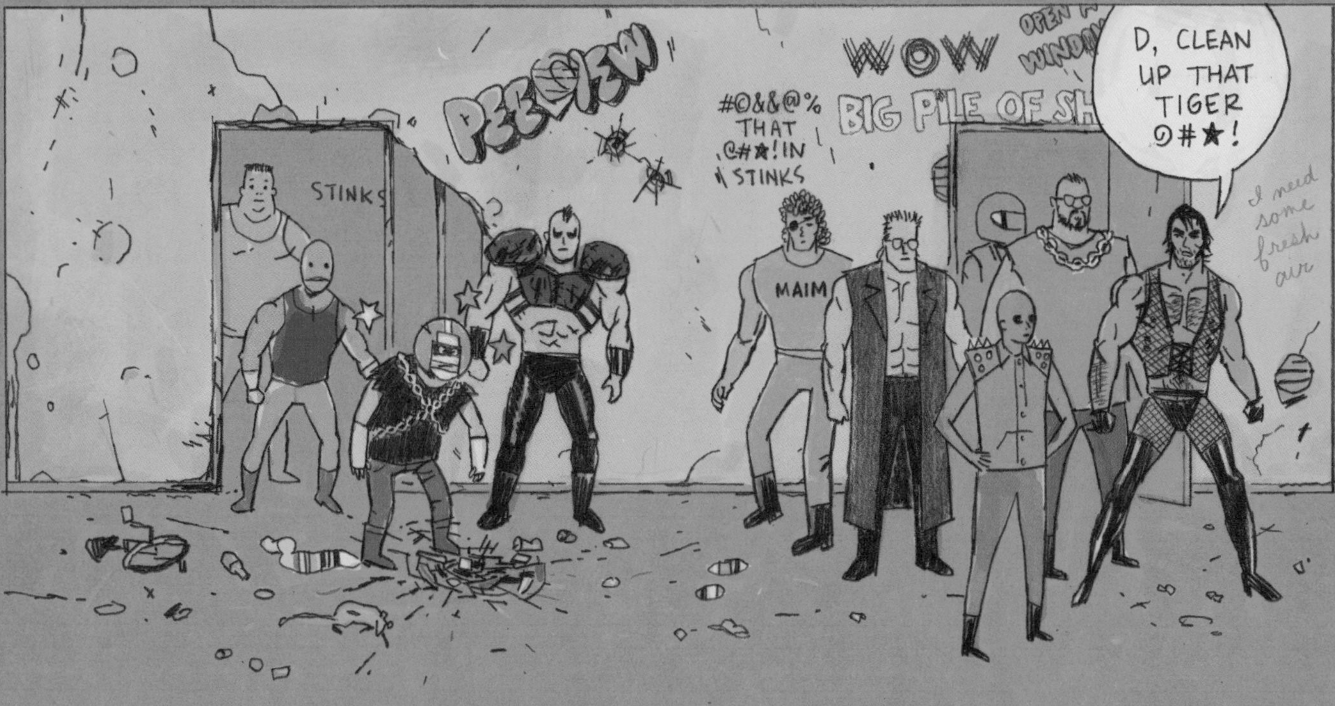
STINKS
WOW
#©&&@% THAT @#★!IN STINKS
D, CLEAN UP THAT TIGER @#★!
I need some fresh air
MAIM

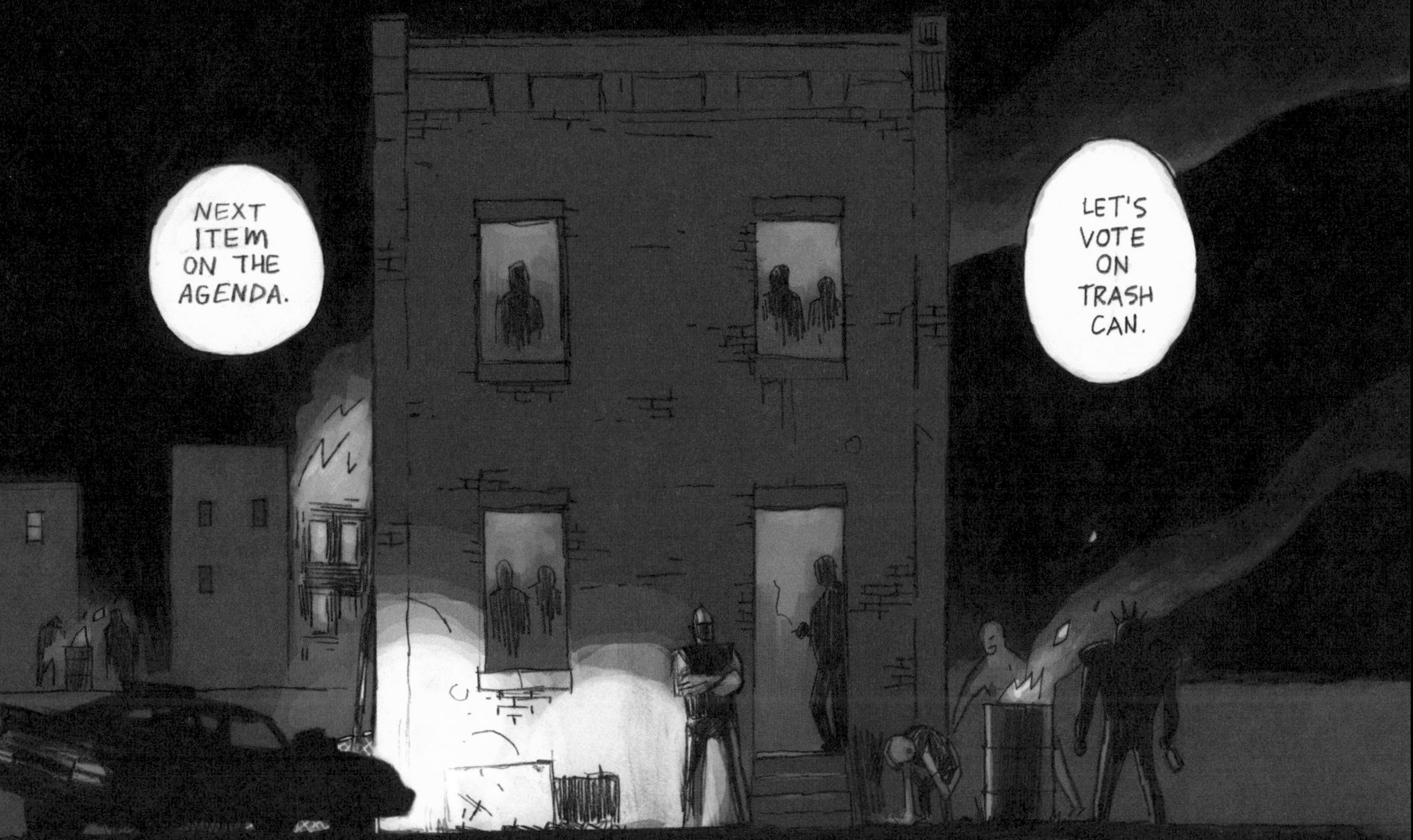
NEXT ITEM ON THE AGENDA.
LET'S VOTE ON TRASH CAN.

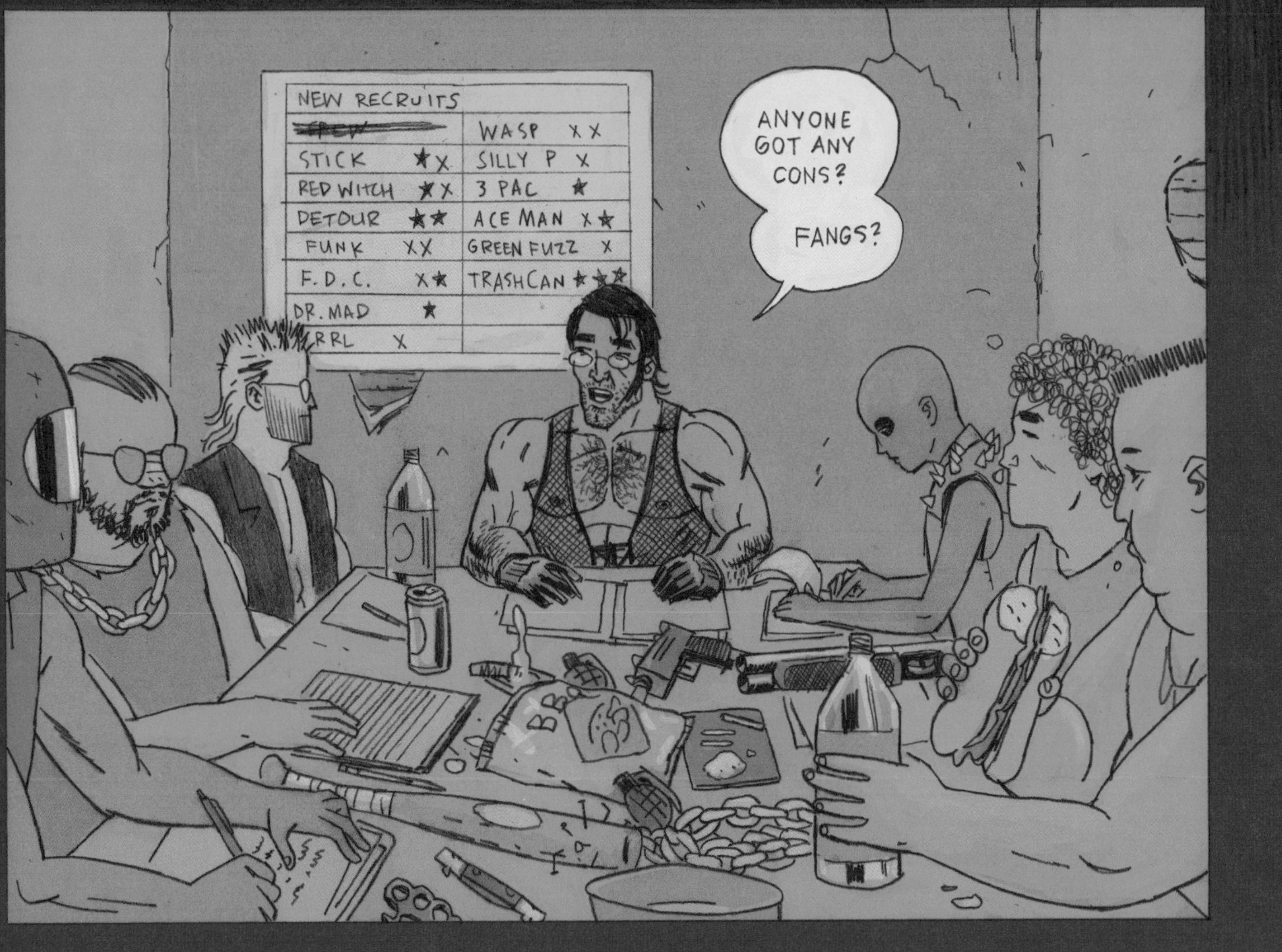
NEW RECRUITS
STICK ★X
RED WITCH ★X
DETOUR ★★
FUNK XX
F.D.C. X★
DR. MAD ★
RRL X
WASP XX
SILLY P X
3 PAC ★
ACE MAN X★
GREEN FUZZ X
TRASHCAN ★★★
ANYONE GOT ANY CONS?
FANGS?

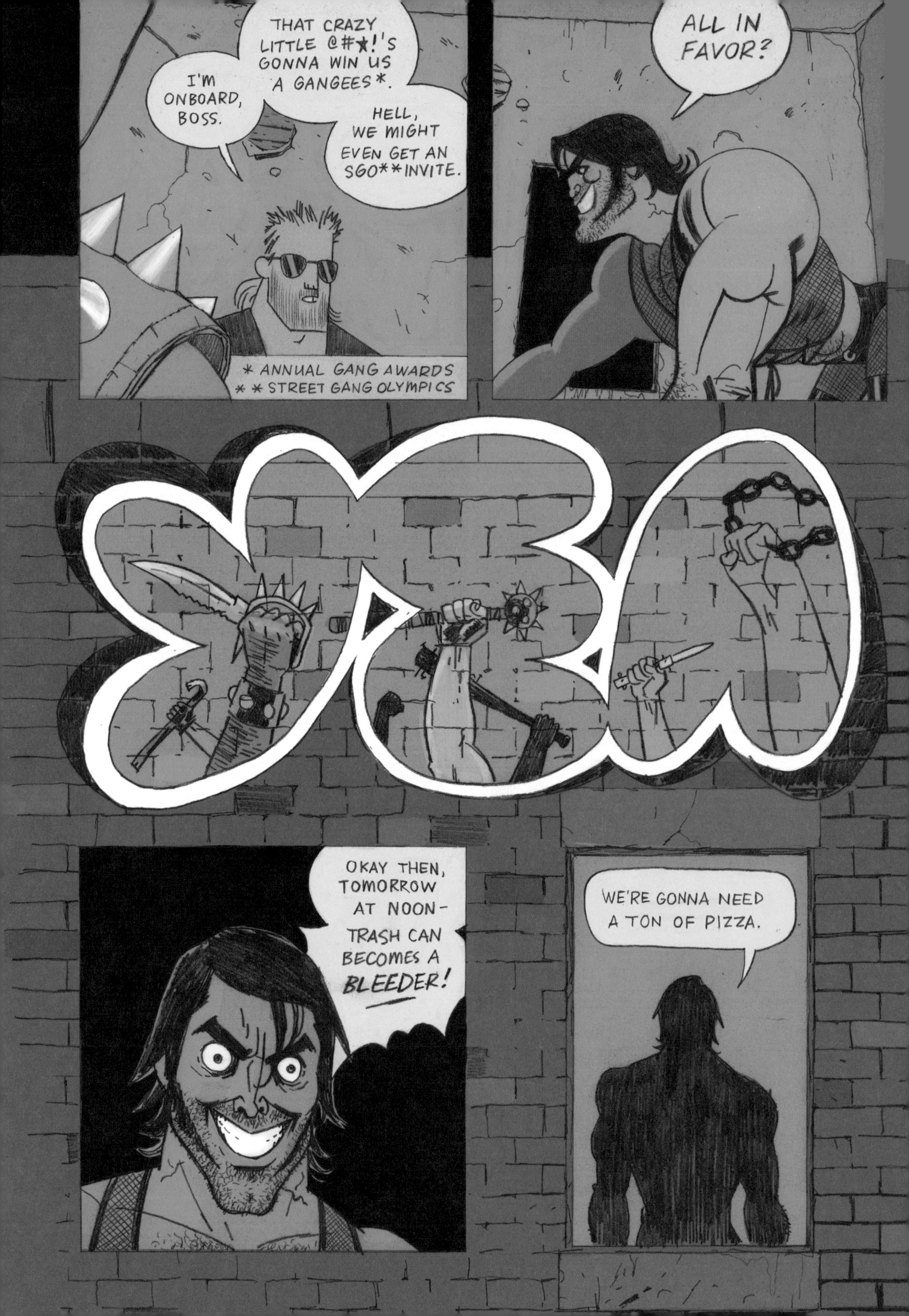
I'M ONBOARD, BOSS.
THAT CRAZY LITTLE @#★!'S GONNA WIN US A GANGEES*.
HELL, WE MIGHT EVEN GET AN SGO**INVITE.
* ANNUAL GANG AWARDS
** STREET GANG OLYMPICS
ALL IN FAVOR?
OKAY THEN, TOMORROW AT NOON- TRASH CAN BECOMES A BLEEDER!
WE'RE GONNA NEED A TON OF PIZZA.

NOON, TOMORROW

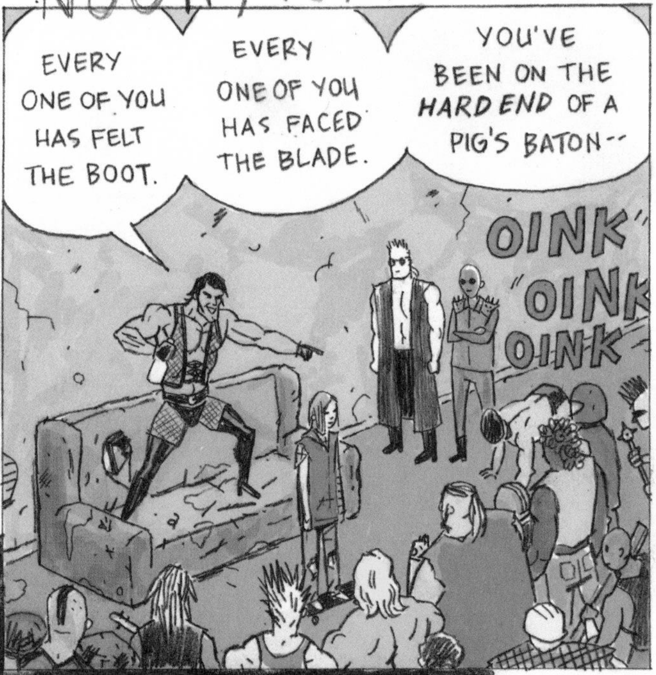
EVERY ONE OF YOU HAS FELT THE BOOT.
EVERY ONE OF YOU HAS FACED THE BLADE.
YOU'VE BEEN ON THE HARD END OF A PIG'S BATON--
OINK" "OINK OINK

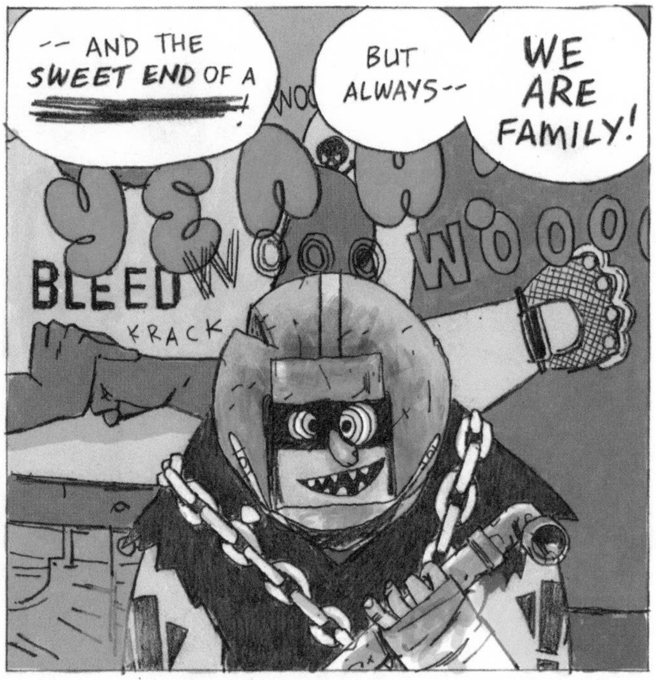
-- AND THE SWEET END OF A [redacted]
BUT ALWAYS--
WE ARE FAMILY!
YEAH
BLEED
KRACK
WOOO

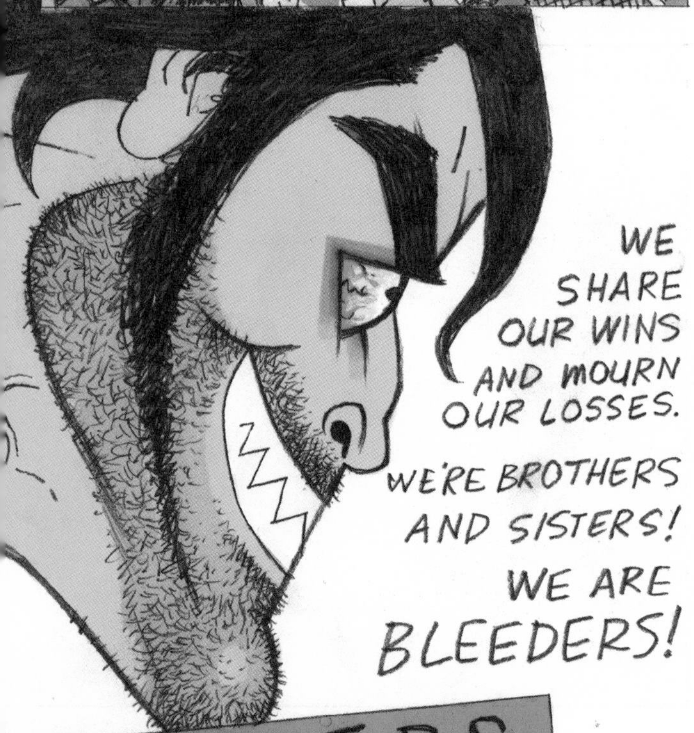
WE SHARE OUR WINS AND MOURN OUR LOSSES.
WE'RE BROTHERS AND SISTERS!
WE ARE BLEEDERS!

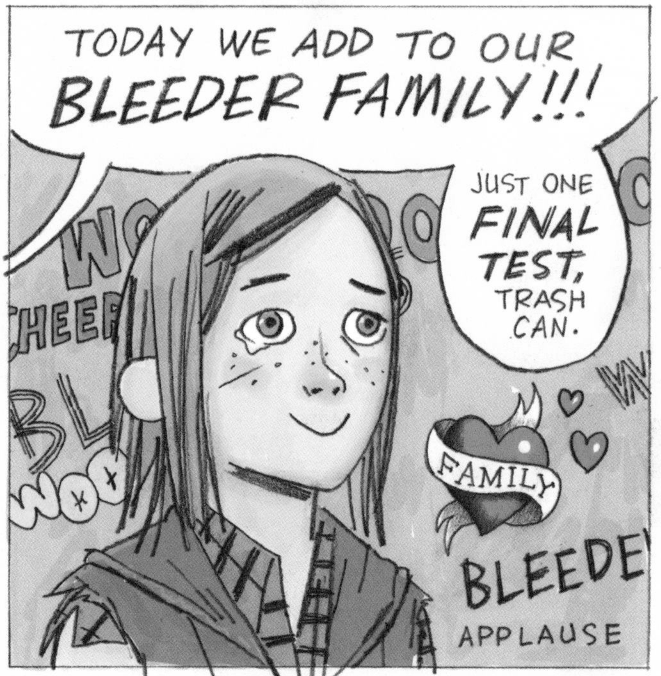
TODAY WE ADD TO OUR BLEEDER FAMILY!!!
JUST ONE FINAL TEST, TRASH CAN.
FAMILY
BLEEDE
APPLAUSE

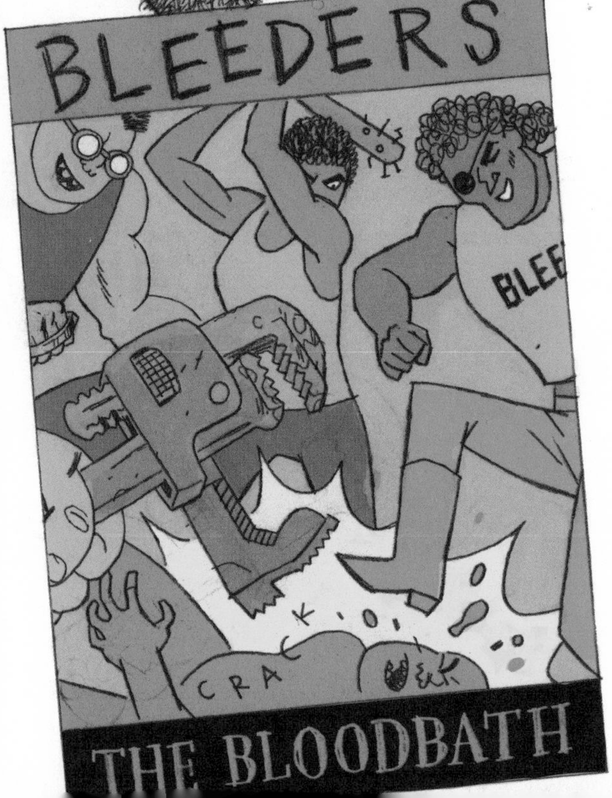
BLEEDERS
BLEE
CRA
THE BLOODBATH

THE BLOODBATH 53

The initiation to become a BLEEDER *is the* BLOODBATH, *a.k.a. the Baptism of Blood.*

Gang members attack the initiate for two minutes. If the new recruit survives, it proves they are tough enough to be a BLEEDER. *The* BLOODBATH *earned its name because the recipient ends up a bloody mess.*

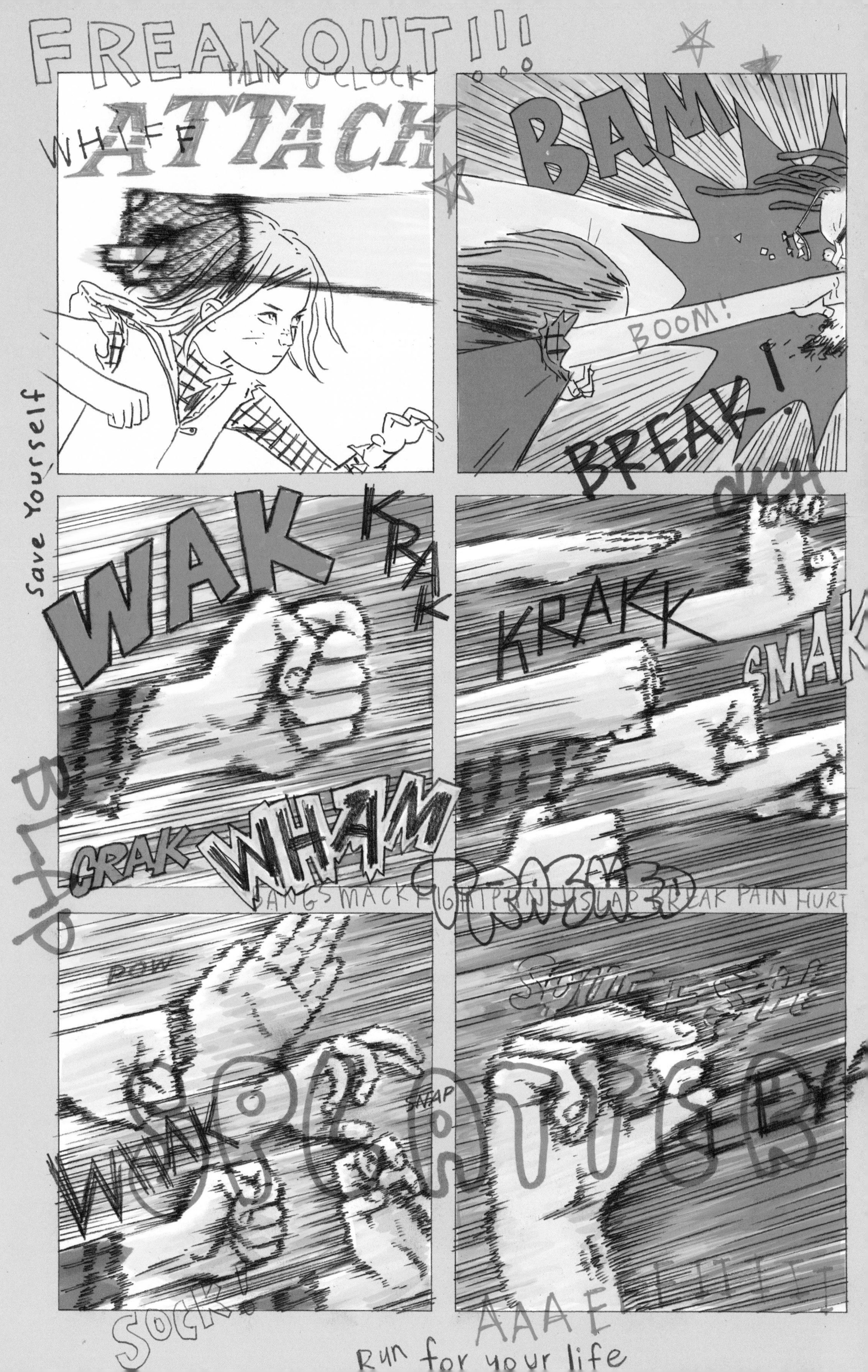
FREAKOUT!!!
WHIFF
BAM
BOOM!
BREAK!
Save Yourself
WAK
KRAK
OUCH
KRAKK
SMAK
CRAK
WHAM
BANG SMACK FIGHT PUNCH SLAP BREAK PAIN HURT
POW
SNAP
WHAK
SOCK!
AAAEIIIII
Run for your life

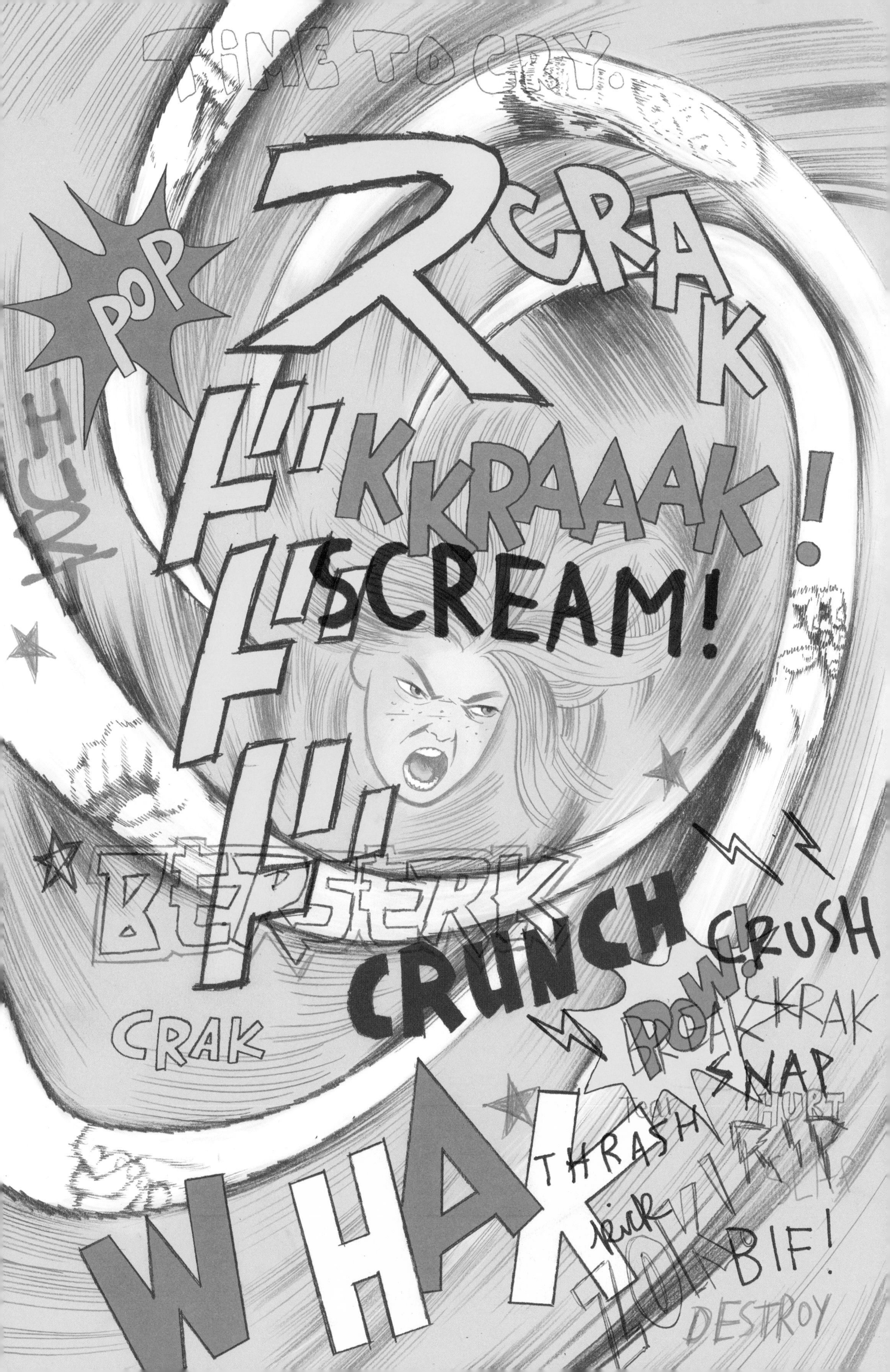

TIME TO CRY.
POP
CRAK
KKRAAAK!
SCREAM!
BERSERK
CRUNCH
CRUSH
CRAK
POW!
KRAK
SNAP
HURT
THRASH
WHAK
BIF!
DESTROY

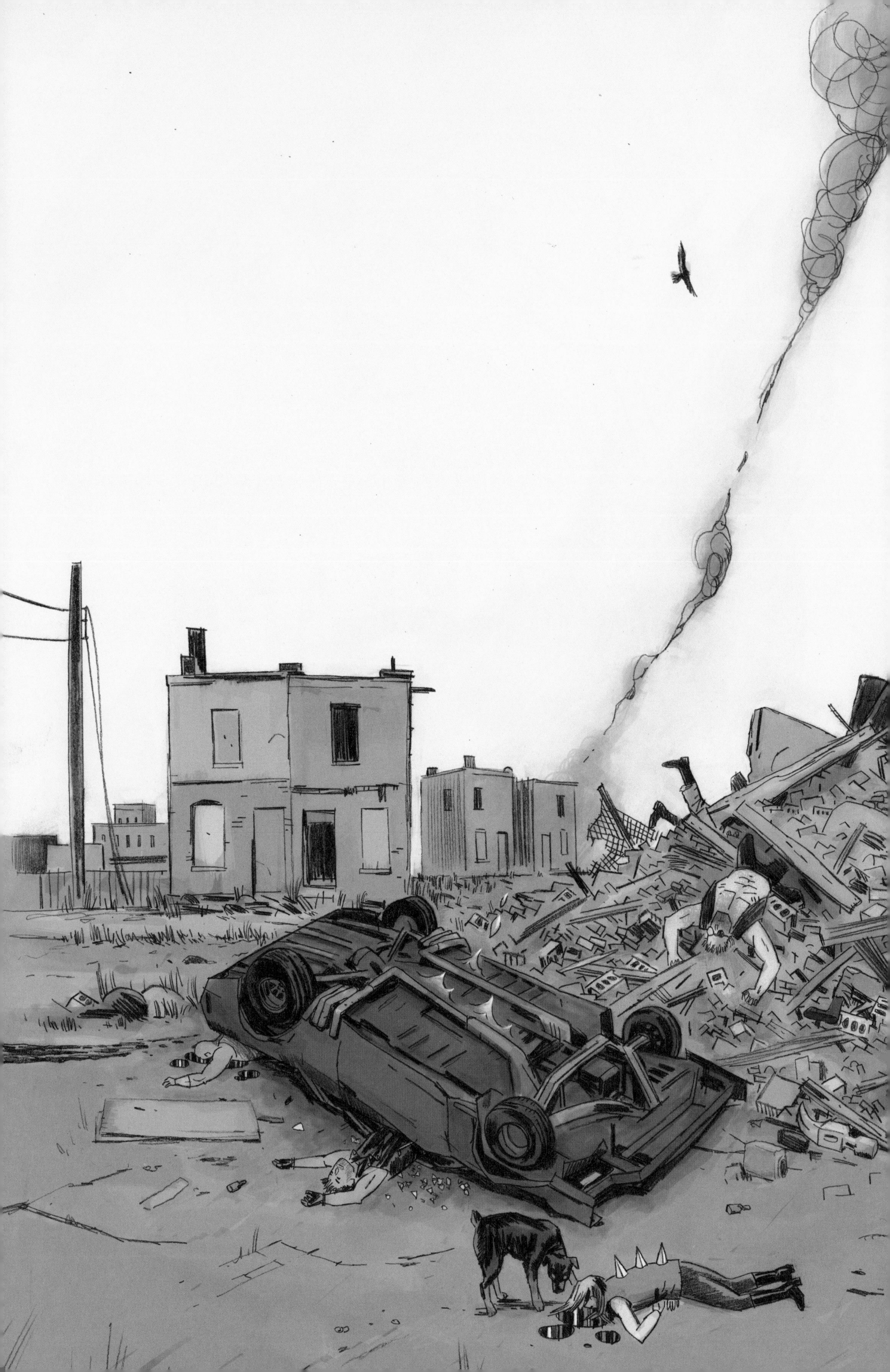

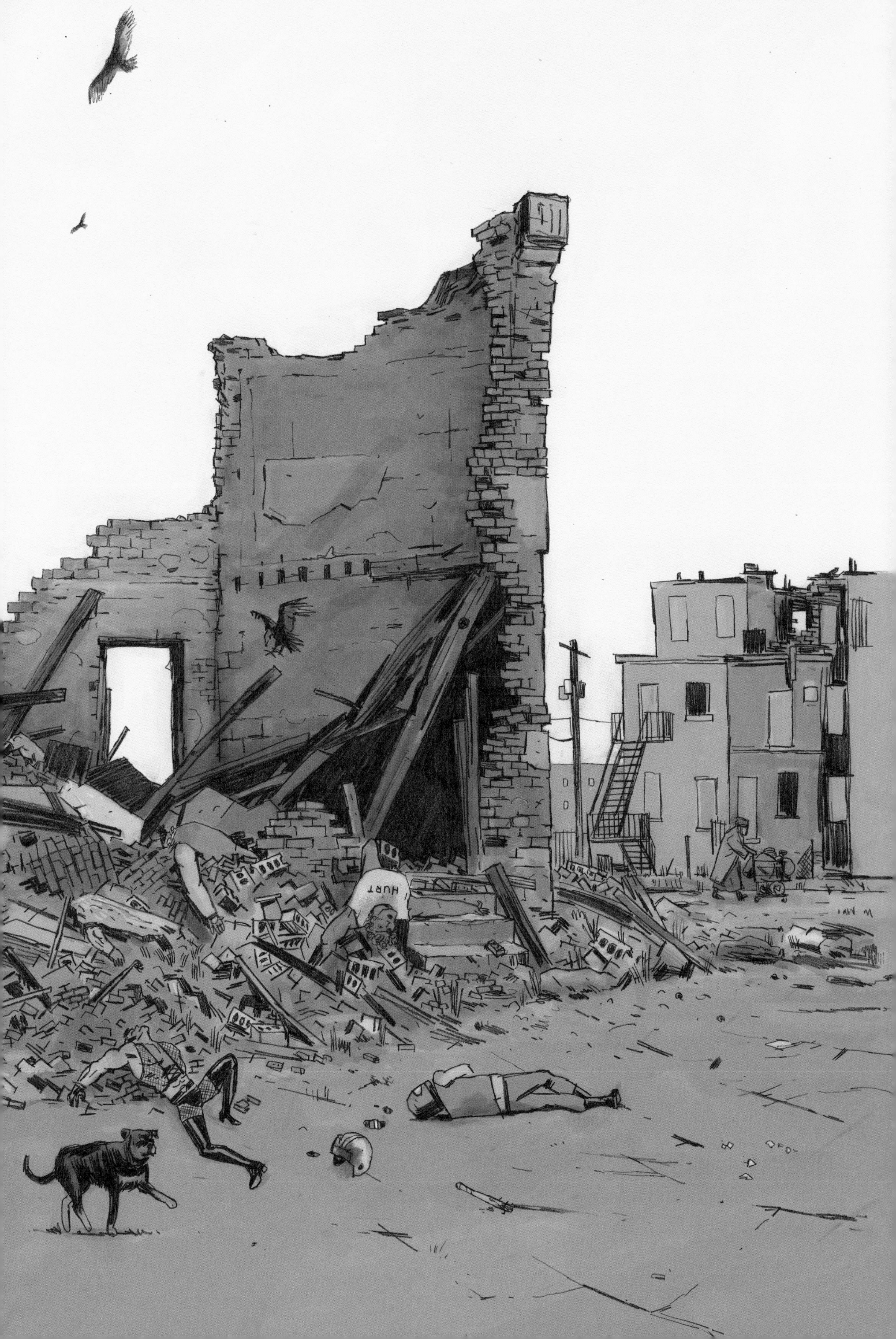
HURT

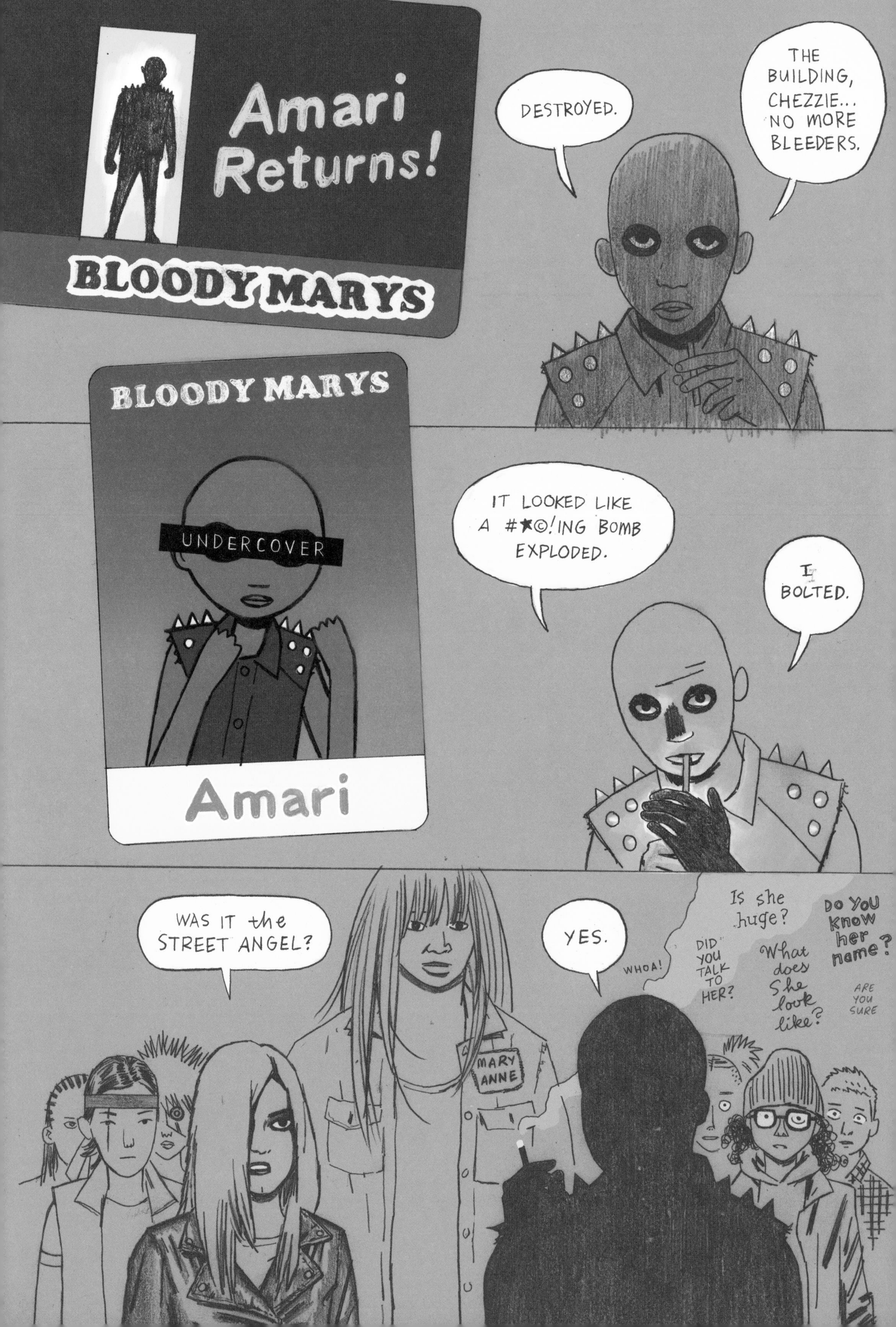
Amari Returns!
BLOODY MARYS
DESTROYED.
THE BUILDING, CHEZZIE... NO MORE BLEEDERS.
BLOODY MARYS
UNDERCOVER
Amari
IT LOOKED LIKE A #★©!ING BOMB EXPLODED.
I BOLTED.
WAS IT the STREET ANGEL?
YES.
WHOA!
DID YOU TALK TO HER?
Is she huge?
What does She look like?
DO YOU know her name?
ARE YOU SURE
MARY ANNE

BOOK CLUB / CLASSROOM DISCUSSION QUESTIONS

??

1. In the Street Angel Gang, Jesse Sanchez joins a violent street gang. Have you ever been part of a group or gang of bad influences? Why did you join that group and how did you get away from it (or are you still part of it)?

2. What would your gang be called? What would your colors be? And who would be your biggest rivals?

3. A lot of young people join gangs to feel like they belong, what are some alternatives to gangs that you can do to find friends and have fun?

4. Vests are really cool - true or false? Bonus: What is better, a denim vest or a leather vest?

5. Do you like Amari? Why or why not? Where does Amari fit in the pantheon of sleeveless heroines?

6. Would you be friends with Jesse? Would you be friends with Street Angel?

7. Are all gangs bad? Can you think of examples of a good gang?

8. What is the main mistake the Bleeders make in their recruitment of Jesse?

9. What would your event be at the Street Gang Olympics?

10. Who would win in a fight, a motorcycle gang, a street gang, a mafia gang, or gangrene?

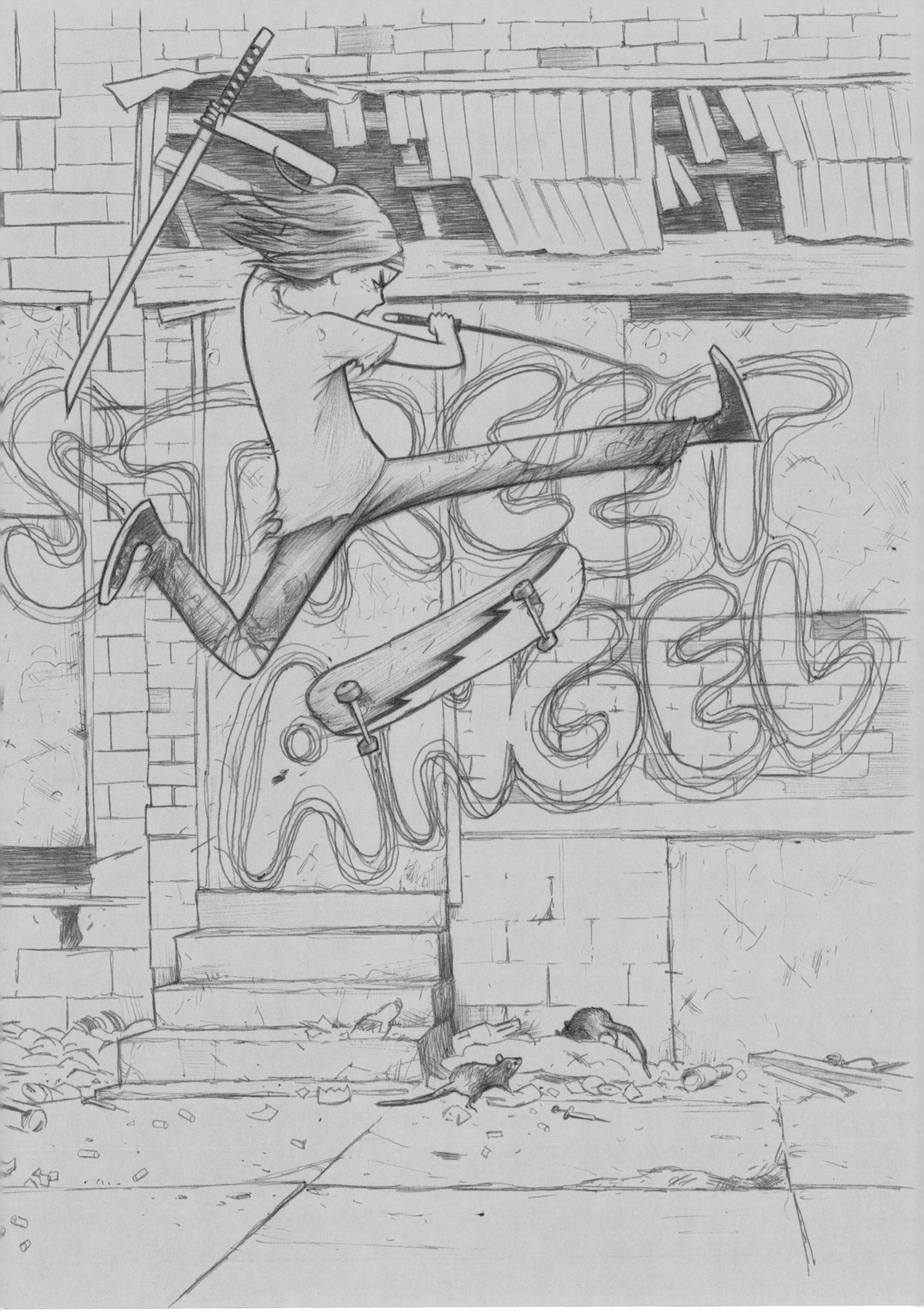

Drawing for Jenn Woodall's zine *Fight 2*

Writing *the Street Angel Gang*

We co-write over email, Google docs, phone, and sometimes IRL at weekly meetings. Our process is organic. Sometimes it begins with a character, a scene, or a concept and evolves through brainstorming and revisions.

Below is the text from the original "draft" of *the Street Angel Gang*. It is from January 2014. According to the revision history, the digital file has been revised 71 times.

Facing is the first page of revision 71. I printed it, stapled it together, and drew it. Editing continued, but it was done on the script or to the artwork.

a colorful multicultural 80s street gang is sitting around their lair.

they're slightly beat up but their leader has been killed in the latest rumble.

they want revenge...but they can't go leaderless.

they have a competition to see who gets to be the new leader (break dancing, knife throwing, doing a report or play about their respective culture, etc).

the newly elected leader decides that he knows why they lost the last fight. not diverse enough. so they set out to find their missing piece.

montage of gang members presenting their applicants.

the last one brings jesse out and everyone is impressed (no one else thought to bring a girl) although there's at least one very obviously a girl among the gang dressed like a dude.

they interview her...ask about her street cred, her background...and they're all kind of feeling the orphan girl vibe.

they tell her joining this gang is like joining a family. we might not all get along (lots of high fives/ hand slapping) but we totally got your back (etc etc).

but we gotta seal the deal with blood.

the group sets upon her to beat her up/fulfill the "set upon" admissions policy.

Jesse destroys them, having no idea that this is part of the initiation process.

the end.

(inside cover and page 1)

01

The gang sign (readable by the comic reader) is in the foreground, right side - page 01.

SIGN: IF NOT YOU, WHO?

If you believe this neighborhood needs a gang,
you can't help but believe that it needs Bleeders.
Don't look over your shoulder. After all, with your
education, ambition and dreams, you have a
personal stake in the future of this city.
And a duty to serve it.

BLEEDERS
Bleed all that you can bleed.
<snack provided>

Last line, small print - "snacks provided" (this may be centered on the comic page for emphasis).

Behind the sign pole, we see the neighborhood. It looks like Fallujah.

The color palette is the same as the opening credits to the Pink Panther.

In the middle ground (left part of page), Street Angel flies through the air (right to left). She's engaged with a man-sized spider monster. The spider monster bleeds green blood from a couple severed legs and gashes on its body. Street Angel's legs are doing an aerial skateboard move and her arms are swinging swords wildly. She's not covered in green blood yet.

In the background, we see a gang kid - Big D hanging another flier on another pole. Big D's oblivious to the Street Angel action behind him.

PAGE 02

02
Big D steps back from the pole. He takes a moment to admire his work. He takes a pull on a beer.

03
He bends down to pickup his box of supplies (more signs, tape, another beer). From behind him (unseen/obscured by him).

JESSE (off panel): What kind of snack?

04
Guy, turning, frightened by the surprise. A little girl, two swords crossed on her back, stands on a skateboard. We see Jesse from behind. She's covered in green grossness - blood from the spider monster.

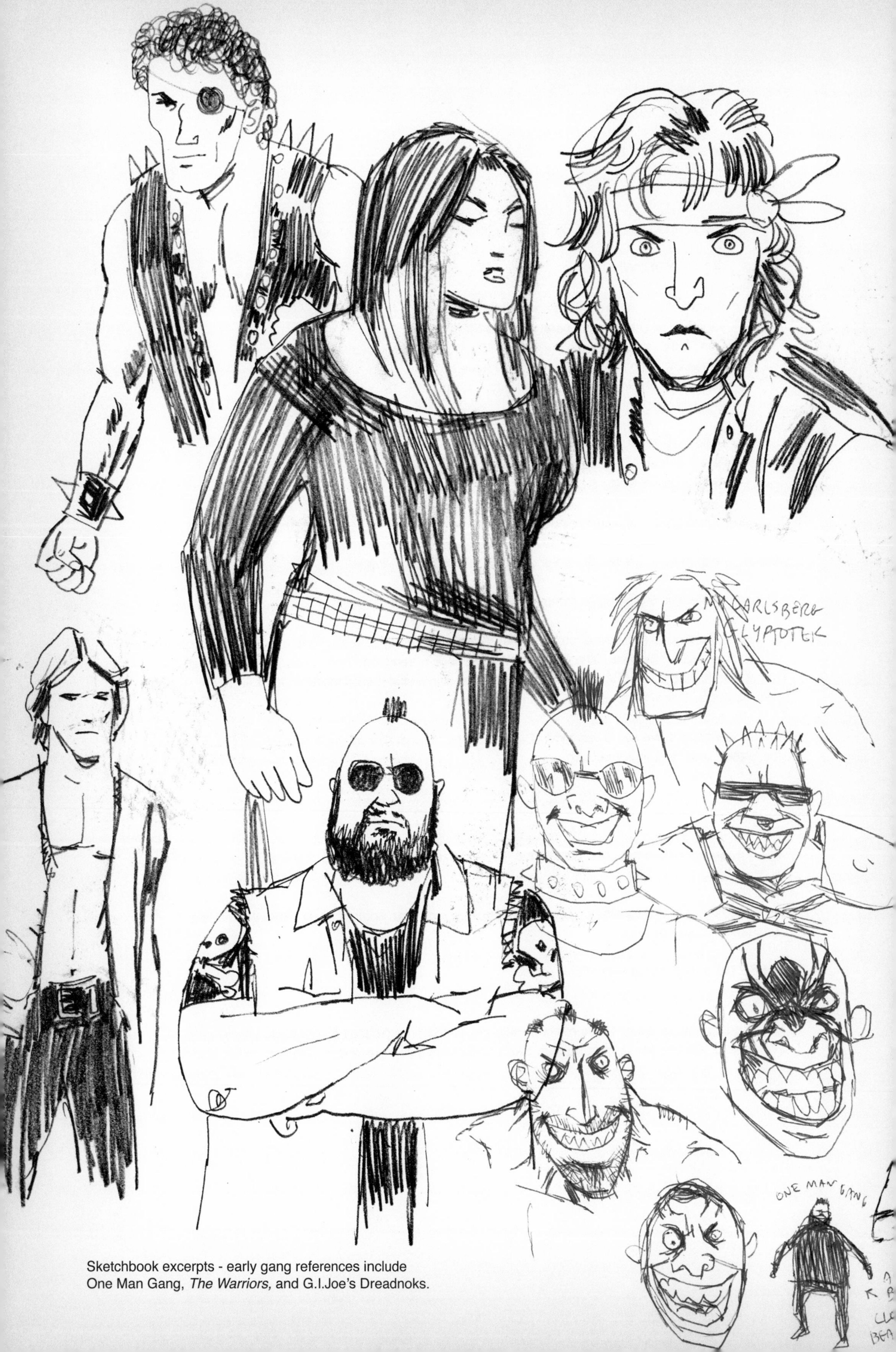
NY CARLSBERG GLYPTOTEK
ONE MAN GANG

Sketchbook excerpts - early gang references include
One Man Gang, *The Warriors,* and G.I.Joe's Dreadnoks.

1st Annual Gang Draft

Let me tell you something about gangs, folks. I'm gonna be real here for a second. I've just done the word/writing equivalent of not just reversing my cap to indicate seriousness, but I've also spun my chair around so I have to straddle it (that the back of the chair provides a handy arm rest is just straight up icing). The only thing I know about gangs is from what I've seen on TV and movies (so, nothing). With that as my lead in, here's my gang fantasy draft. Mostly what I learned from this effort is that I don't watch a lot of anything with any kind of gang in it:

1st Annual Gang Draft (feel free to write in with your own, far more superior, gang draft):

Leadership:
Chains Cooper from *Stone Cold*
Jed Eckert from *Red Dawn*
Side Kick:
Muttley from Wacky Races
Brains:
Theo from *Die Hard*
Thelma from *Scooby Doo*
Muscle:
Jessica Yang from *Super Cop*...technically a cop undercover in a gang, but I'll allow it.
Sloth from *Goonies*
The Humungus from *Mad Max: The Road Warrior*
Buffy
Foot Soldiers:
Jesse and James from Team Rocket
Brion James as Brion James in most things.
Al Leong as Al Leong in most things
Comic Relief:
Cholla, leader of the Black Widows in *Any Which Way But Loose*
Zed McGlunk from *Police Academy 2*

Yep.

Brian Maruca

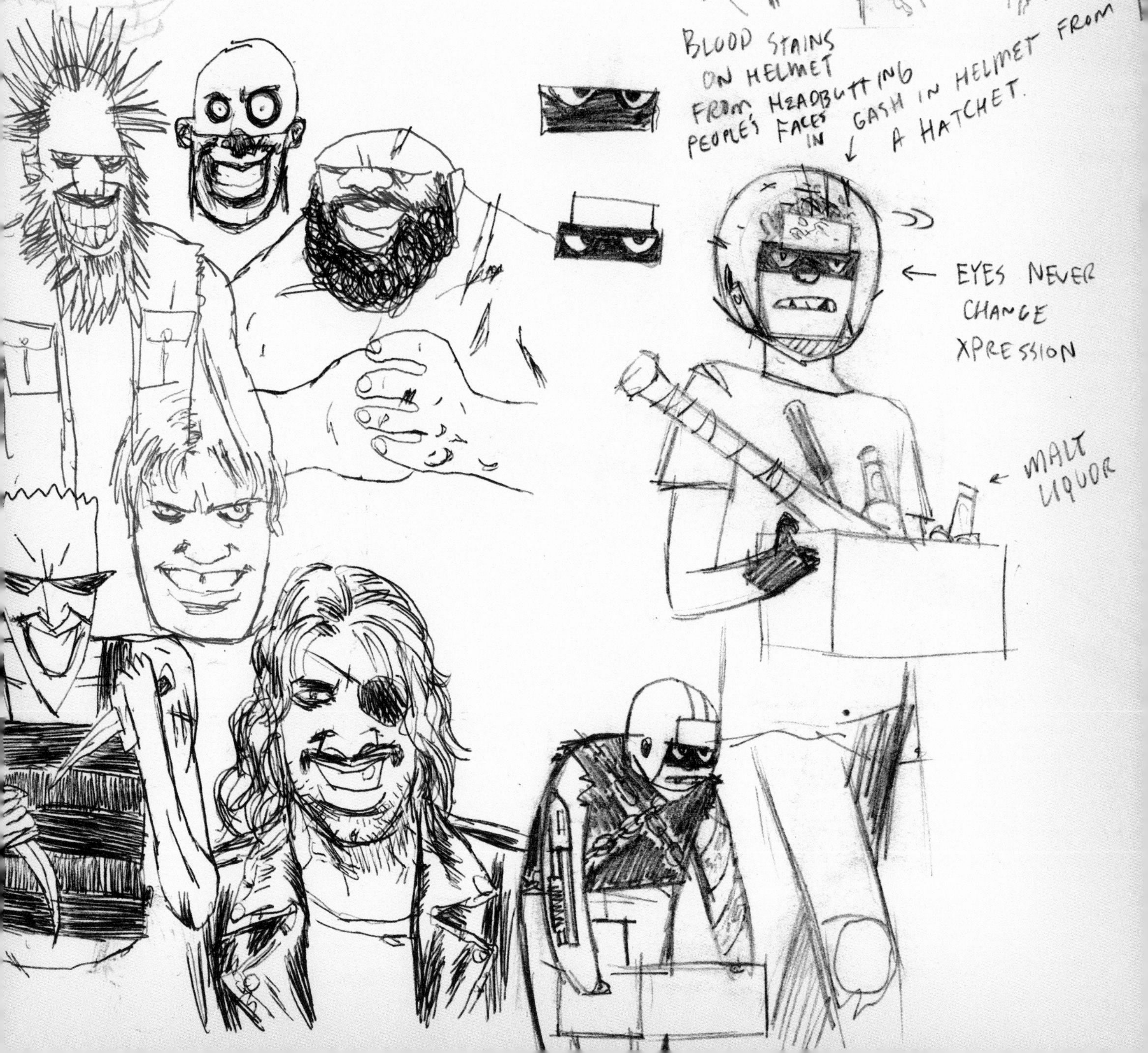
BLOOD STAINS ON HELMET FROM HEADBUTTING PEOPLE'S FACES IN
GASH IN HELMET FROM A HATCHET
EYES NEVER CHANGE XPRESSION
MALT LIQUOR

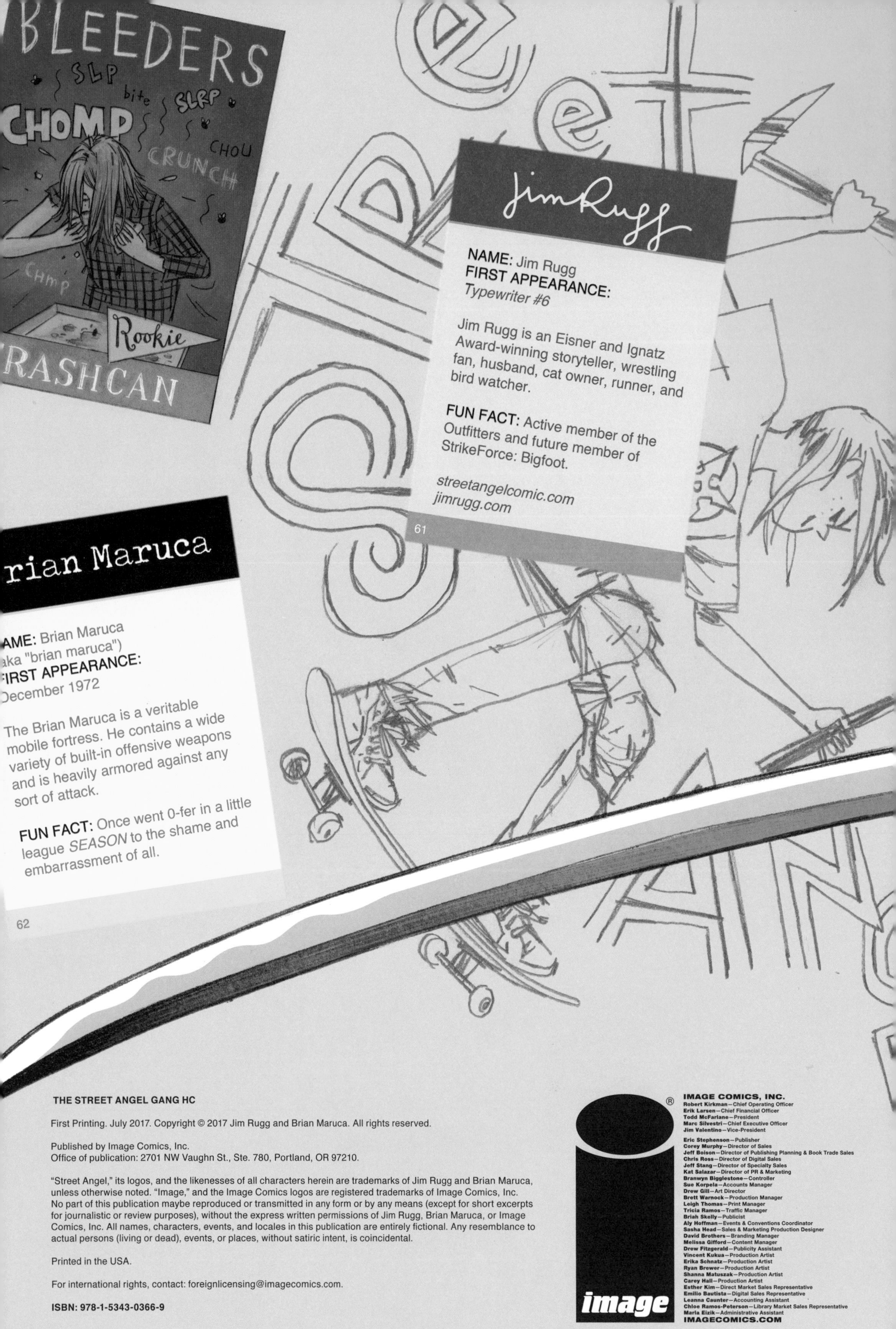
BLEEDERS
SLP
bite
SLRP
CHOMP
CHOU
CRUNCH
CHMP
Rookie
RASHCAN
Jim Rugg
NAME: Jim Rugg
FIRST APPEARANCE:
Typewriter #6
Jim Rugg is an Eisner and Ignatz Award-winning storyteller, wrestling fan, husband, cat owner, runner, and bird watcher.
FUN FACT: Active member of the Outfitters and future member of StrikeForce: Bigfoot.
streetangelcomic.com
jimrugg.com
61
rian Maruca
AME: Brian Maruca
aka "brian maruca")
FIRST APPEARANCE:
December 1972
The Brian Maruca is a veritable mobile fortress. He contains a wide variety of built-in offensive weapons and is heavily armored against any sort of attack.
FUN FACT: Once went 0-fer in a little league SEASON to the shame and embarrassment of all.
62

THE STREET ANGEL GANG HC

Published by Image Comics, Inc.
Office of publication: 2701 NW Vaughn St., Ste. 780, Portland, OR 97210.

Printed in the USA.

For international rights, contact: foreignlicensing@imagecomics.com.

ISBN: 978-1-5343-0366-9

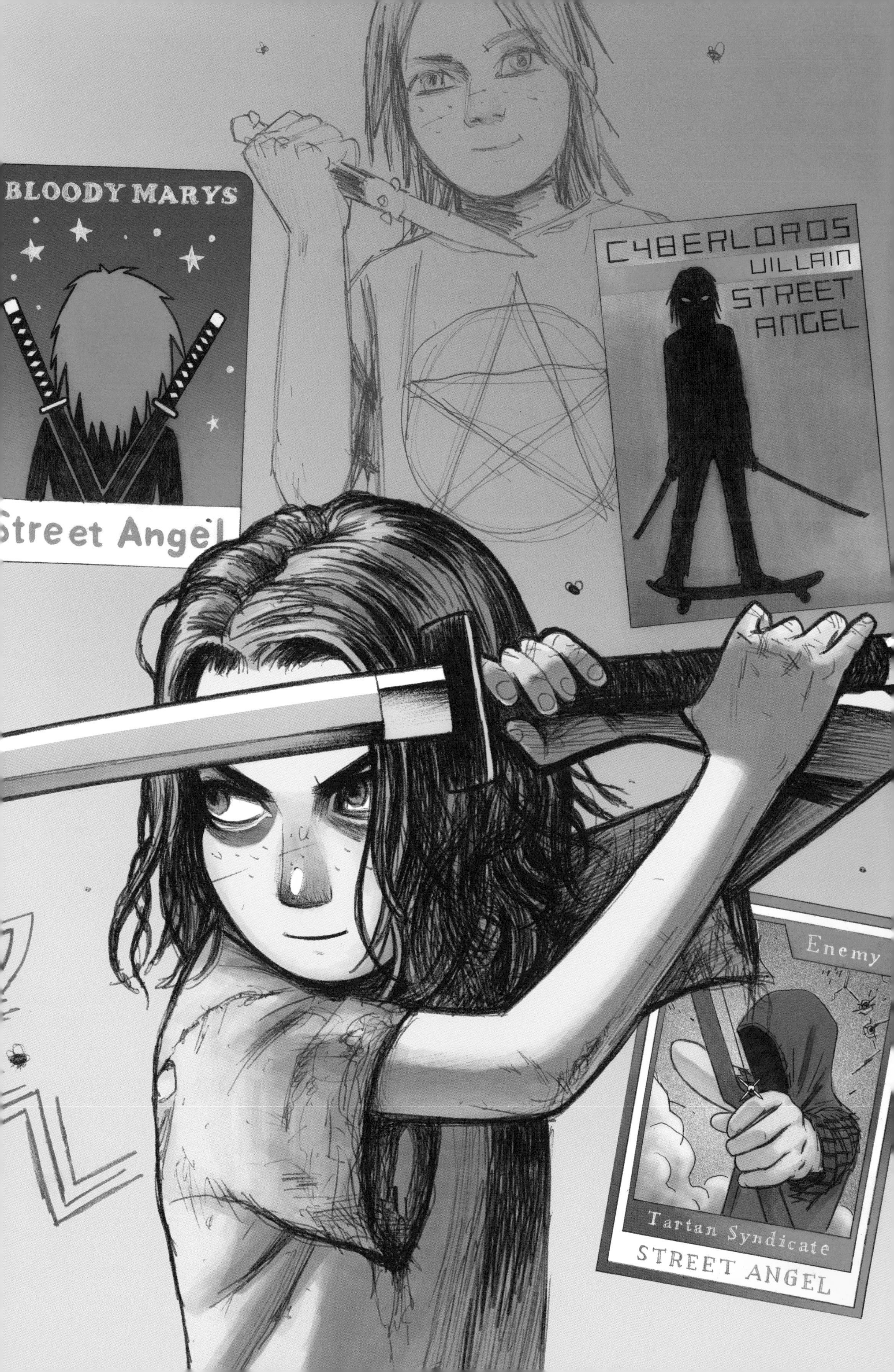
BLOODY MARYS
Street Angel
CYBERLORDS
VILLAIN
STREET
ANGEL
Enemy
Tartan Syndicate
STREET ANGEL

Bell

NAME: Maxine Bell
FIRST APPEARANCE:
After School Kung Fu Special

Jesse's extra-extraverted best friend, Bell is a B+ student and lives with her mad scientist father. She is super loyal and stands up for her friends.

FUN FACT: Bell is unaware that she is a robot.

10

RED KITE

NAME: Rachel King
FIRST APPEARANCE: *Alcatraz, Jr.*

Hoping to catch lightning in a bottle, RK's adopted superhero father, Super Hawk, abandoned her at the circus. Besides traumatizing the young girl emotionally, it kind of worked. She kept the moniker when she struck out to hero on her own.

FUN FACT: Rachel hasn't spoken to Super Hawk in 4 weeks and is making good progress according to her therapist.

11

SUPER Emm

NAME: Emma Smith
FIRST APPEARANCE:
Super Hero for a Day

By the stars in the skies
and by the fish in the seas
with a will that won't die
and by the sharpest of deeds
when you can't escape your latest
 dilemma
look no further than Super Emma!

FUN FACT: Regular Emma is a zombie. The good kind.

14

CHECKLIST 1-30

1. Check Please!
2. Going for a Spin!
3. Papa Don't Preach!
4. Pizza Party!
5. 2-on-1 is No Fun!
6. No Escape!
7. Iya Meets His Match
8. Greaseball Special!
9. Back to Back!
10. Bell
11. Red Kite
12. Bald Eagle
13. Lilith
14. Super Emma
15. The Devil
16. Ninja Cat
17. Afrodite
18. Captain Alpha
19. Treasure Chest
20. Street Angel
21. Dr. Pangea
22. Becky Dumpling, Baby Sitter
23. Serpentina
24. NINJA6000
25. The Moon
26. ENIXAM
27. Nun Chuck
28. T2T3
29. Vanman
30. Organ Grinder

59

SKATEBOARD

FIRST APPEARANCE: 1940s/1950s

The skateboard was created by surfers who wanted to ride the waves when they couldn't get to the beaches. It's been skinning knees, breaking bones, and pissing off the man ever since.

QUESTIONABLE FACT:
A skateboard can also be called a scooter!

53

BALD EAGLE

NAME: Anthony Eagle
(aka: Armstrong)
FIRST APPEARANCE:
Street Angel #1

The Bald Eagle believes that he on has two degrees of separation from Kevin Bacon. His skateboarding ski are enhanced by his low center of gravity but hindered by his inability to kick.

FUN FACT: He has road rash on 75 of his body and will be happy to sho it to you.

12

AFRODITE

NAME: Aliyah Jefferson
FIRST APPEARANCE:
After School Kung Fu Special

Principal by day, shaping young kids' minds in Wilksboro's toughest (and only) high-security public school ~ and ~ vigilante by night, protecting the city from the men who would do it harm.

FUN FACT: She will mess you up with facts or fists.

17

NINJA CAT

NAME: Paul Shultz
FIRST APPEARANCE: unknown

Meow meow meow meow meow meow meow meow meow meow meow meow meow meow meow meow meow. Purr. Meow meow meow meow meow meow meow meow meow meow mew.

FUN FACT: Ninja Cat spelled backwards is Tac Ajnin.

16

Treasure Ches

NAME: Timbre Trunks
FIRST APPEARANCE:
Art and the Orphan

Timbre has the ability to warp reality and withdraw from the mystic realm any item that she needs. She has no idea how it works.

FUN FACT: She's very tired of pointing out she "gets what she needs not what she wants" from the mystic realm.

19